PICTURES OF THE PAST

Lydia's Aunt Mattie goes on a cruise with her friend Joel, and asks Lydia to run her guesthouse near Ullswater. But Joel's nephew Luke Carstairs is also there to help, and Lydia resents his interference. She also resents his interest in her family history, and his reticence to talk about his own background. And what is the mystery about the old photograph album? How can Lydia find the truth, and cope with her growing attraction to Luke?

SPECIAL MESSAGE TO READERS

This book is published under the auspices of

THE ULVERSCROFT FOUNDATION

a registered charity (No. 264873 UK)

Established in 1972 to provide funds for research, diagnosis and treatment of eye diseases.

Examples of contributions made are:—

A Children's Assessment Unit at Moorfield's Hospital, London.

Twin operating theatres at the Western Ophthalmic Hospital, London.

A Chair of Ophthalmology at the Royal Australian College of Ophthalmologists.

The Chair of Ophthalmology Research at the Great Ormond Street Hospital For Sick Children, London.

You can help further the work of the Foundation by making a donation or leaving a legacy. Every contribution, no matter how small, is received with gratitude. Please write for details to:

THE ULVERSCROFT FOUNDATION

The Green, Bradgate Road, Anstey,
Leicester LE7 7FU, England.
Telephone: (0116) 236 4325

In Australia write to:

THE ULVERSCROFT FOUNDATION

c/o The Royal Australian and New Zealand
College of Ophthalmologists,
94-98 Chalmers Street, Surry Hills,
N.S.W. 2010, Australia

JEAN M. LONG

PICTURES OF THE PAST

Complete and Unabridged

LINFORD
Leicester

First published in Great Britain in 2008

First Linford Edition
published 2008

British Library CIP Data

Long, Jean M.
    Pictures of the past.—Large print ed.—
Linford romance library
    1. Family secrets—Fiction
    2. Lake District (England)—Fiction
    3. Love stories
    4. Large type books
    I. Title
    823.9'14 [F]

    ISBN 978–1–84782–453–0

Published by
F. A. Thorpe (Publishing)
Anstey, Leicestershire

Set by Words & Graphics Ltd.
Anstey, Leicestershire
Printed and bound in Great Britain by
T. J. International Ltd., Padstow, Cornwall

This book is printed on acid-free paper

An Unexpected Guest

The breakfast rush was over, and Lydia had just waved goodbye to a party of hikers who were setting off for the hills. The Metcalfs in the family room were getting themselves organised for a trip into Keswick, and the two elderly ladies in room five were going on a coach tour, so out of all the guests currently staying at Hill House, only the couple in room four had yet to decide what to do with themselves for the day.

Glad to have a few minutes to herself, Lydia stepped out into the garden to get a breath of fresh air and to admire the stunning Lakeland view. It was a glorious May morning, and the fells, clothed in muted shades of green and brown, stood out boldly against the skyline. But needs must and, with a sigh, she turned and went back indoors.

As she cleared the table by the bay

1

window in the dining-room, she couldn't help but yawn. It had been a long journey the previous day from Kent to Hill House, her aunt's guesthouse near Ullswater, and then Aunt Mattie had insisted on filling her in with everything from A to Z before satisfying herself that her niece really was capable of running the place for her while she was away on a cruise.

It had been mid-evening before Lydia had managed to slip away for a while to visit friends in the village, then she'd been up again at the crack of dawn to wave goodbye to her aunt and her aunt's friend and neighbour, Joel Norris, as they set off together on their holiday.

She was stifling another yawn when a discreet cough made her whirl around.

Observing her from a table in the far corner of the room was a youngish, broad-shouldered man with a thatch of brown hair.

Startled, she hurried over to him. He must have booked in while she'd been out the previous evening. She was a bit annoyed that her aunt hadn't told her there'd been a late arrival.

'I'm so sorry — I'm afraid I didn't notice you there. What can I get you?'

He gave her a charming smile. 'The menu would be helpful. I've been sitting here for at least ten minutes.'

Lydia coloured. 'Then I apologise Mr . . . er . . . '

'Carstairs — Luke Carstairs.'

She handed him a menu and he scrutinised it carefully.

'Scrambled eggs, mushrooms, bacon and tomatoes, I think,' he said at last. 'Oh, and a big pot of coffee, please.'

As she turned away he called after her. 'Have you had your own breakfast yet?'

She shook her head.

'Then why don't you join me?'

She hesitated. 'Er, well, I've got a mountain of washing-up to do and Mrs Dalton — the daily help — isn't due for another half-hour or so, and her daughter, Gemma, who helps part-time, is off today. Besides, it isn't really

3

Hill House policy to . . .'

'Have breakfast with the guests?' he finished for her. 'But you see, I'm not actually a guest.'

She stared at him, her heart missing a beat. Was he an intruder? Anyone could have just walked in. After all, she had left the door wide open.

She registered that he was a tall, powerfully-built man, probably in his mid-thirties, with rugged features and a determined set to his jaw.

'I'm surprised your aunt didn't mention me to you,' he said, frowning. 'I'm Joel Norris's nephew.'

Relief swept over her.

'So you're Joel's nephew! Aunt Mattie has told me about you, of course! She said you'd be staying in Willow Cottage to supervise the builders while your uncle's away.'

He smiled and, getting to his feet, held out a large hand.

She took it and was immediately aware of a slight shiver dancing along her spine.

4

'You weren't here when I arrived at Uncle Joel's last night. I popped over to introduce myself to Mattie and she suggested that, since I'll have some spare time on my hands, it would be good if I could help you shoulder some of the burden of running this place. She said she'd speak to you about it.'

Lydia felt even more annoyed with her aunt — and Luke Carstairs.

'Well, she didn't speak to me about it. And it looks to me as if you're here to get your breakfast made for you rather than to be helpful. Anyway, I'm quite capable of running the place without your assistance.'

'Good. So, how about some breakfast before I fade away . . . ?'

'Fat chance of that!' she told him rudely, surveying his large frame and catching a hint of rippling muscles beneath his T-shirt.

But his grin was infectious, and she didn't want to stand there all day arguing with him, so she bit back a sharp retort and, hurrying back to the kitchen, set about scrambling eggs.

★　★　★

He was engrossed in the daily paper when she went back with his breakfast. She set the plate of food before him and he eyed it appreciatively before picking up his knife and fork and attacking it with enthusiasm. He paused long enough to ask, 'So where's yours?'

'I couldn't carry any more,' she retorted, stacking dirty crockery on a tray before going back through to the kitchen, returning a few minutes later with her own breakfast.

'Now, let's get a few things straight,' she said firmly. 'Neither Joel nor Aunt Mattie mentioned anything about you coming here this morning, whether to scrounge a free breakfast or to keep an eye on me or whatever.'

His brown eyes flickered with amusement. 'Ah, well, I always did like the element of surprise. Seriously though,

6

your aunt did say she'd speak to you about me giving you a hand.'

'Well, she hasn't,' Lydia assured him.

As they munched in silence for a few moments, she wondered how on earth she came to be eating breakfast with this stranger, who obviously knew more about her than she did about him.

Aunt Mattie might have warned her, she thought again, irritably.

Well, if Luke Carstairs thought he was going to barge in here and start throwing his weight around, then he was mistaken.

She decided to adopt a coolly polite approach, while attempting to find out more about him.

'So, how long are you planning to stay in Silverdale?' she asked.

'Like yourself, until your aunt and my uncle return from their holiday. This is lovely bacon.'

'I'm glad you like it. Well, you can see for yourself that everything's under control here, so you can go off and do whatever it is you've got to do.'

'Thanks, I will,' he replied pleasantly. 'When I've finished my breakfast.' And he poured himself some more coffee.

Matilda Lawson's niece was not at all how Luke had imagined she would be. He'd expected a rather frumpy spinster, but this spirited young woman was far from that and he realised that he was keen to learn more about her. A shaft of sunlight streaked her hair with gold and lit her face so that, far from being ordinary, as he had at first thought, he realised that she was really quite pretty. Her large blue-grey eyes were lovely — long-lashed and expressive.

Skilfully, he got her to relax by encouraging her to talk to him about some of the places he could visit in the locality. He felt quite disappointed when Mrs Dalton put her head round the door.

'Sorry I'm a bit late, Lydia, but my hubby needed a button sewing on his shirt at the last minute, would you believe? I'll get on with the dishes shall I?'

Lydia got to her feet, glad of an

excuse to escape from the room.

In the kitchen, Mrs Dalton, a round, jolly little person, tied an apron round her ample waist, rolled up her sleeves and proceeded to tackle the washing-up.

'Why your aunt doesn't see fit to invest in a dishwasher, I'll never know.'

'Because she's already got one,' Lydia quipped. 'You!' She picked up a tea cloth.

It wasn't until later that morning when she went into the office to look at Aunt Mattie's list of things to do, that she found the memo that had been stuck to it.

'In case I forget to tell you, Joel's nephew, Luke, is coming round for his breakfast while the builders are in at Willow Cottage. He's offered to lend you a hand, if need be, so don't hesitate to ask him. Sorry you didn't get to meet him yesterday.'

Lydia reflected it was a pity she hadn't found the note before. It might have prevented her from making such a complete fool of herself! Her cheeks were warm as she remembered the way she had spoken to Luke Carstairs. On the other hand, her aunt's note made it sound as if it were Luke who'd taken the initiative to offer to help out at the guesthouse, rather than her aunt asking him to keep on eye on Lydia. Hmm . . . she collected a shopping bag and set off to the village.

* * *

'I don't understand it,' she told Ginny Bassett who ran the Silverdale Stores and had been her friend for many years. 'Why would a young chap want to spend his spare time helping out at a B & B? Especially when he looks the outdoors type. You'd think he'd want to get out walking or something, rather than hang around Hill House.'

Ginny finished pricing some pots of preserves.

'If you want my opinion, I think you're making too much of it, Lyddie.

After all, surely Mr Norris's nephew is at Willow Cottage to keep an eye on his uncle's builders? So, he's not going to be under their feet all day but, at the same time, he'll not want to be too far away, will he? Look, I'm just about to close for lunch so why don't you come into the back and we'll have a proper chat — we hardly had time to say more than 'hello' when you dropped by last night, did we?'

As they sat over lunch in the cosy kitchen, Ginny continued, 'If this nephew is prepared to oversee things at Willow Cottage and help you out as well, then he could prove to be an asset.'

'Hmph!' Lydia said, waving her toasted sandwich in the air. 'He'll be wanting to move into Hill House next!'

'And would that be such a bad thing? After all, if I were you, I wouldn't relish sleeping in a house full of strangers.'

'Well, he's another one, isn't he? I don't know a thing about him,' Lydia pointed out.

'So,' Ginny said reasonably, 'I don't suppose he knows too much about you either.' She snapped her fingers. 'You know, that could be why he's so keen to poke his nose into the guesthouse. Your aunt and his uncle have gone off on this cruise and they've barely known each other for five minutes.'

Lydia stared at Ginny as her words sank in.

'You could well be right,' she said slowly. 'I hadn't thought of it like that. After all, I've seen Joel several times, but Luke Carstairs only met Aunt Mattie for the first time — and briefly at that — last night. But she isn't a gold-digger if that's what he's thinking! Actually, I've got my own reservations about her friendship with Joel Norris — how do we know what his intentions are? He seems a nice enough guy on the surface but . . .'

'Well, there you are then. You're each of you suspicious of the other's relations! He's just sussing out your Aunt Mattie and your family.'

She selected an orange from the fruit bowl.

'Help yourself — more tea?'

Lydia passed her mug and, taking an apple, bit into it.

'So, what do your parents make of your aunt's growing relationship with Mr Norris? After all, she was married to your Uncle Ted for such a long time,' Ginny asked as she poured the tea.

'Oh, they don't seem at all concerned, but then my mother's very preoccupied helping my sister-in-law with her new baby, and Dad's in his own little world, busy with work, as usual.'

'And what about your sister?'

'She's a bit non-committal. But she'll be coming up here next week to join me now that Maisie's school holidays have started.'

Lydia thought of her young niece and smiled.

'Anyway, if there's anything to suss out, then Jenny'll find it.'

'But Mr Norris seems such a lovely

chap — kind and considerate towards your aunt — always pleasant to everyone. Surely you wouldn't begrudge the pair of them a little happiness?'

Lydia frowned. 'That's exactly what my parents said, but I can't help but be worried. After all, Aunt Mattie seems a bit vulnerable. It's very difficult to imagine her with anyone else after Uncle Ted because they always seemed so right for one another.'

Ginny shook back her mane of dark hair and said in her level-headed way. 'And that's the problem, isn't it? You're bound to view Joel Norris with suspicion because, in your eyes, no-one else could possibly live up to your Uncle Ted. But if your parents aren't worried then why should you be?'

Lydia shrugged, finding it difficult to put her doubts into words.

'Oh, I don't know — this cruise is just so out of character. Aunt Mattie's always seemed such a sensible sort of person and a creature of habit. Apart from visiting her sister in Yorkshire and coming to us in Kent once in a blue moon, she and Uncle Ted never went anywhere beyond Morecambe Bay in a caravan. And now to go off on a cruise with a man who's virtually a stranger!'

Ginny's hazel eyes were thoughtful. 'Well, I expect your uncle left her comfortably off so why shouldn't she enjoy spending some of her money? After all, she's worked her socks off running the guesthouse by herself since your uncle died and, as you say, apart from visiting her sister once or twice, she hasn't been anywhere else — not even Morecambe Bay!'

'Oh, I don't know — perhaps you're right, Ginny!'

Her friend said astutely, 'I suppose you're not burying yourself up here and involving yourself in Mattie's affairs because you've got problems in your own life down in Kent?'

'Why would you think that?' Lydia demanded, eyes widening.

'Well, pardon me for mentioning it, but you've scarcely had two words to say about that gorgeous hunk of a boyfriend of yours . . . you haven't split up, have you?'

Lydia swallowed. 'No — not exactly. There are a few issues, but I'll tell you all about them another time.'

She was uncomfortably aware that Ginny could read her like a book, but she wasn't ready to talk about Trent — not yet. She needed some space to think things through.

She finished her apple, drained her mug and got to her feet.

'Thanks for lunch and the chat, Ginny. I feel much better now. And I only came by for the bacon and yoghurt — oh, and I'd better take some more eggs. I'm pretty good at breaking them at the moment and not everyone wants scrambled!'

★ ★ ★

It was only a short step along a winding track past the church before she was back in the lane that led up to Hill

16

House, and she hummed to herself as she walked, pausing to look at the lambs frolicking in a nearby field.

As she entered the guesthouse, she came to an abrupt halt at the sight of Luke Carstairs clutching a holdall and talking with a bewhiskered, elderly gentleman who was carrying a rather battered suitcase.

'Ah, Lydia! Mr Jones has turned up on the off chance you might have a spare room. Apparently, he's stayed here once or twice before. I've checked with Mrs Dalton and room six is available for a few days.'

Lydia opened her mouth to make a cutting remark, then remembered Mr Jones just in time.

Stretching out a hand, she welcomed the new guest, and Luke Carstairs escorted the elderly gentleman up the stairs. Just as if he owned the place, she thought crossly.

She was waiting for him when he reappeared a few minutes later.

'I think it's high time you and I had a

chat,' she told him icily and opened the door leading into the small office. He scooped up the holdall that he'd left in the hall and followed her inside.

She didn't sit down, not wanting him to have the advantage of towering over her, but perched on the desk instead.

'While my aunt's away I'm in charge here,' she told him firmly. 'She wouldn't have agreed to go on holiday otherwise. You have no right to allocate a room to Mr Jones without consulting me first. In fact, it was absolutely none of your business.'

'But you weren't here and I was,' he pointed out.

She was determined to keep her cool and met his glance unwaveringly.

'I'd left my mobile number written on the pad on the desk — anyway, do I really need to justify myself to you?'

He inclined his head. 'Of course you don't but, actually, I think I've got as much right as you to make a decision.'

She was taken aback. 'And how,

exactly, do you make that out?' she demanded.

'Perhaps it would be better if you waited until your aunt returns from holiday and let her explain . . . '

'Explain what? I haven't got the remotest idea what you're talking about,' she told him curtly.

'No, that's obvious.' He hesitated. 'Well, I don't suppose it'll matter if I tell you. You see, Uncle Joel is having the cottage done up in order to let it out during the summer months when he'll move in here to help your aunt. I expect they'll start offering an evening meal as well as bed and breakfast. It'll be a joint enterprise and so they'll share the profits.'

Everything was moving much too fast for Lydia's liking. A number of thoughts raced through her head, and she wondered whether the man standing in front of her was telling the truth.

'So, what part do you play in all this?' she asked him, watching closely for his reaction.

'The same as you, I would imagine — that of a concerned relative, wondering if my uncle is making the right decision.'

Anger and astonishment filled her, but before she could reply, there was a knock on the door and Mr Jones stood there looking apologetic.

'So sorry to trouble you again, but I haven't any towels or soap in my room and I'd quite like to freshen up.'

Lydia was glad of a reason to get out of the office. Her head was in a complete whirl. Aunt Mattie hadn't breathed a word about this latest turn of events. It looked as if her concern at the speed with which the friendship between her aunt and Joel Norris was developing was fully justified.

Aunt Mattie had been wonderful to Lydia, Jenny and her brother Andrew when they had been children. One year, their father had been seriously ill and Uncle Ted and Mattie had brought the children back to live with them for a few months. They had spent many happy holidays in Silverdale since then and had come to regard it as a second home.

Now Lydia considered it to be her turn to look after Aunt Mattie's interests and ensure that she was all right.

⋆ ⋆ ⋆

When she returned to the office after putting towels and toiletries in room six, Mr Jones was still in there chatting to Luke. She left them to their conversation — about cricket — and went through to the kitchen to put away her shopping. Which was where Luke found her a few minutes later.

'Look, I realise this is a bit of a nerve, but I'm going to have to throw myself on your mercy.' He indicated the holdall.

'I take it you're planning to move in,' she said.

He gave a short laugh. 'Are you a mind reader or something? I was hoping it might be possible for me to stay here for a few days, because the electricity is off in the cottage while the builders are doing alterations to the kitchen. Obviously, if you object, then I'll have to see if I can find somewhere else to stay.'

'You and Joel have got it all worked out between the two of you, haven't you?' Lydia told him. 'Did you mention to Aunt Mattie that you might need to stay here?'

He looked surprised. 'Well, no, how could I when I didn't realise what was happening until this afternoon? Uncle Joel did say something about the electrics, but it didn't register, I'm afraid. I can't have been listening properly.'

She sat on a stool and stared at him. There was a roguish twinkle in his eyes and she realised he reminded her of a naughty school boy.

'I ought to send you packing,' she told him sternly. 'Give me one good reason why I should let you stay?'

He grinned. 'Because it means I'll be on hand to help out here.'

'Huh!' she said. 'So, having given Mr Jones the last available spare room in the house, where exactly do you propose to sleep? I positively draw the line at the sitting-room sofa, and I've absolutely no intention of letting you near Aunt Mattie's room. Perhaps you're proposing I should move out to accommodate you!'

To her annoyance, he laughed. 'Now there's an idea. Perhaps your friend, Ginny, would put you up — mind you, I'm not sure how organised I'd be at cooking the breakfasts. Anyway, there's no need for that. You obviously haven't been told . . . '

'Told what?' she demanded irritably, wondering what else Aunt Mattie had kept from her.

'Come on, I'll show you!' He picked up the holdall again.

Mystified, she followed him to the top of the house.

'If you're thinking of the attic, then

don't; it's full of dust and junk,' she told him.

'Was, you mean!'

He pushed open a door at the top of a winding staircase and she gasped. The attic had been transformed into an attractive bedroom with white walls, built-in wardrobes and a double bed with a blue and white duvet and matching curtains.

She stepped past him on to a thick, inky blue carpet and gazed around in astonishment.

'When did all this happen?'

'A couple of months back, apparently. Your aunt hired the same builders who're making the alterations to Willow Cottage.'

Lydia crossed to the small window and peered out. It gave a wonderful view of verdant fields full of sheep, and of the towering fells beyond. The attic had been the place where Andrew, Jenny and herself had played as children and now it had all changed.

After a few minutes, she turned to

find Luke watching her, a curious expression etched on his face.

'So, where did all the stuff go?'

'What stuff?' It was his turn to look puzzled.

'All the things that were up here — the toys, the pictures and dressing-up clothes.'

'I dunno — you'll need to ask your aunt, unless . . .'

He slid open one side of the built-in wardrobe to reveal that it was really a walk-in cupboard with hanging space, a long mirror and a chest of drawers inside. He closed it and tried the other side, to reveal countless boxes piled high and a couple of tea chests all filled to overflowing.

'There you are — that solves that mystery. But how come you're so well acquainted with the contents of your aunt's attic? After all, you're only here for a week or two every year.'

'You seem to know an awful lot about me and my family,' she said sharply. 'I've known Aunt Mattie all my life and she and Uncle Ted moved from their small cottage and came to live here when I was quite young, because her parents had died by then — it had been the family home for several generations — and her sister, Janet — who's a teacher and has never married, before you ask — was living and working in Yorkshire and quite settled there, with no intention of moving back to the Lake District.'

'How intriguing!' he murmured and she wondered if he was being sarcastic.

'As children, my brother, sister and myself spent some wonderful holidays up here. We actually lived here for several months, on one occasion, when my father was seriously ill. My aunt and uncle looked after us and we attended the village school. The attics were our playroom.'

'So Mrs Lawson's husband, Ted, was your father's brother?'

She nodded. 'His older brother by quite some years. He asked Aunt Mattie out after buying a bouquet from her when she was working in a florist's shop.'

She sat down on an old rocking chair, lost in thought, and he went over to the window seat.

'It's a very romantic story, actually. He went into the shop to buy some roses for a girl he was taking out, but she stood him up, and so the next day he returned to the florist's, gave Aunt Mattie the roses and asked her out instead. It was a whirlwind romance. After they got married, they moved into a pretty little cottage and stayed there for a number of years — although Uncle Ted worked away a lot of the time.'

Lydia's uncle had been in show business — a stand-up comedian.

Luke listened to all this intently. 'So I take it your uncle met your aunt quite by chance when he was passing though Silverdale in the course of his work. Your family are all from down south, aren't they?'

'Well, no. My father's family are from

up here — it's my mother's side of the family who come from Kent. My parents met at York University and, when they got married, lived in Yorkshire for several years. That's where the three of us were born. It wasn't until my mother's father died that we moved down south — to be nearer my grandmother.' Lydia paused. 'So now you know about my family history; what about yours?'

He got his feet. 'Oh, that'll keep for another time. Tracing one's ancestors is quite a popular pastime these days, but it isn't always a good idea to rake up the past, is it?'

The remark sounded heartfelt and she said simply, 'I suppose some people might find it difficult.'

He nodded. 'So, have I got your permission to stay here until Willow Cottage is habitable again?'

She sighed. 'Oh, I suppose so. Mind you, I shall expect you to earn your keep and to really lend a hand if you're staying here.'

He pulled a face. 'You're a Miss Bossy Boots, aren't you?'

They descended the top flight of stairs and, when they reached the first landing, he opened the door to what had once been a linen cupboard, to show a newly-fitted shower room.

'You see, I'll have all mod cons.'

Things had certainly been happening since the last time Lydia had visited Hill House. And how come Luke Carstairs seemed to know everything that was going on before she did?

She found herself wondering if there were any more surprises in store for her.

What Does Luke Want?

The next few days fell into a comfortable routine, thanks to Aunt Mattie's copious notes. Lydia was quite pleased with the way things were going and, in spite of any misgivings she might have had about him, Luke had kept himself very much in the background.

In any case, taking charge of Hill House wasn't too arduous a task, because Lydia had helped out before on several occasions.

She was taking a breather one afternoon, enjoying a cup of tea in the sun lounge when Luke came to join her.

'So, what's on the agenda for this afternoon?'

'As you can see, I'm having a tea break. Most of the guests are out, so I'm not needed until breakfast tomorrow morning.'

'Good — then how about we go for a walk? It's too beautiful an afternoon to be stuck indoors . . . And can you spare a cup of tea? I've been over to the cottage and it's quite dusty.'

She had already realised that he was a man who was used to getting what he wanted.

'Go on then — take the pot and top it up and fetch yourself a mug from the kitchen.'

He returned a few minutes later with a loaded tray. 'I found a nice big fruitcake in the tin so I've cut a couple of slices — hope that's OK?'

'Make yourself at home, why don't you?' she muttered.

'Thanks, I will,' he replied, her sarcasm apparently lost on him, although she thought she detected a glint in his eyes. He settled himself in a basket chair and crossed his legs.

'Your aunt's a good cook! So what was your uncle like?'

'Oh, he was kind and generous to a fault. He died about four years ago.

That's when my aunt expanded the B & B business.'

He sipped his tea. 'Needs the money, does she? Do I take it he didn't leave her very well provided for?'

'This is a big house to maintain,' she said evasively, determined not to be drawn into any discussion about her aunt's affairs. 'And it can be lonely living on your own.'

He surveyed her, head on one side. 'That was heartfelt — do you live on your own?'

'As a matter of fact, yes — not that it's any of your business.'

'You're very prickly. Bad experience?' he asked, giving her a searching glance.

She felt the colour rising to her cheeks and bit her lip.

'As I've said, it's none of your business! Look, can we stop discussing me? Or I might just be tempted to start directing questions at you!'

He raised his eyebrows. 'That could prove interesting. So what would you like to know?'

She helped herself to a slice of cake. 'Well, for a start, why are you so interested in finding out everything you can about my aunt's affairs?'

His eyes narrowed. 'What makes you think I am?' he countered.

But before she could reply, there was a knock on the door. It was the elderly sisters from room five.

'So sorry to disturb you, Miss Lawson. We bought some teacakes from the village store,' one of them said.

'And we wondered if we could toast them for our afternoon tea!' the other one finished, proffering a bulging paper bag.

To Lydia's surprise, Luke sprang to his feet, took the teacakes and said, 'But, of course! Why don't I see to them for you? And I expect you'd like a nice pot of tea to go with them?'

The elderly ladies beamed at him and Lydia realised that Luke was intent on proving himself to be Mr Nice Guy.

★ ★ ★

About a quarter of an hour later, he came back with another pot of tea for Lydia and himself.

'Hope it was OK, but I gave them a few pats of butter and some strawberry jam. They were very grateful.'

'Just so long as they don't start thinking we're a café.'

No sooner were the words out of her mouth than Mr Jones appeared in the doorway, wearing an apologetic look.

'So sorry to trouble you, but the friend I was hoping to have supper with tonight has got an unexpected engagement that he can't back out of. I don't suppose there's any possibility that you might stretch a point — just this once? Beans on toast would do.'

There was a slight pause while Luke looked at Lydia and winked, so that she felt obliged to say, 'Well, I was intending to have a home-made cottage pie that my aunt left for me in the freezer. There's far too much for one — so you'd be welcome to share it. I usually eat around six-thirty.'

'You're a star,' Luke said, when the old gentleman had gone.

'Too soft by halves,' she told him and downed her tea.

He finished his cake and wiped his fingers. 'Let's go for that walk now, shall we, before someone else comes asking for a favour and, when we get back, I'll help you to prepare the veg to go with that home-made cottage pie.'

'I'll hold you to that!' she warned, eyeing him suspiciously.

It was a beautiful afternoon for a walk. They set off along the lane past Willow Cottage, where the builders were still hard at work, and took the footpath across the fields.

'You see it's not that difficult to be civil to one another, is it?' he said, tucking his arm through hers.

The sudden contact sent unexpected shock waves pulsating through her, so that she caught her breath.

'So, Lydia, what do you do when you're not running a guesthouse?'

'Don't tell me there are things about

me that you don't know!' She was genuinely surprised, imagining that Aunt Mattie would have filled him in. 'I'm a freelance photographer — mainly children and family portraits — animals too.'

It was his turn to look surprised. 'Really? — So that photograph of the cat on the wall in the sitting room — that's your work, is it?'

She nodded. 'And the group portrait of the children above the mantelpiece in the dining-room — the Metcalfs, taken last year. There are a few more of my photographs dotted around, mostly in the bedrooms.'

'But that can't do you much good publicity-wise, if you're based in the south,' he commented.

'You'd be surprised. A lot of the guests who come here are from the south of England or have relatives who live there. We do weddings and school photos and family events, too.'

'We?' he asked. 'So you don't work alone then?'

She shook her head — not wanting to talk about her relationship with her business partner and boyfriend, Trent Symons. She loved her studio in Canterbury with the small flat above it, but was grateful for this breathing space, away from it all, in order to sort out her confused emotions.

She deftly swung the conversation back to Luke. 'So what about you?'

He let go of her arm abruptly. 'Me? Oh, I've got a pad in London and, before you ask, I'm a hotel manager.'

Light began to dawn. No wonder he was so keen to see what was going on here, although she wouldn't have thought it would have interested him that much. In her opinion, there was a world of difference between running a hotel and running a guesthouse.

They stopped to admire the view.

It was idyllic. They were surrounded by fields full of quietly munching Herdwick sheep. In front of them was a gently flowing stream and, beyond that the fells, clad in their rich tones of bronze, green and gold. She wished the walk could go on forever, because when such tranquil beauty surrounded her, her problems seemed to dissolve.

She gave a heartfelt sigh and he stared at her. 'What's wrong?'

'I just wish I could bottle this and take it back home with me. It's so very beautiful, although I expect you're bored out of your skull.'

He shook his head. 'No, I love the countryside and open spaces!' He spread his arms wide about him. 'Although — would you believe it — I've never been to the Lake District before?'

'Then you'll know now what you've been missing.'

He nodded in agreement. 'But now my uncle's finally decided to settle down at long last, I guess we'll be up and down the motorway periodically. I'm certainly impressed with all that I've seen up here — the peace and tranquillity — to say nothing of the spectacular scenery.'

Lydia was only half listening. She was wondering who the 'we' he'd referred to could be. Perhaps he was married? After all, she hadn't thought to ask. Somehow, she found the thought disquieting.

She said brightly, 'You seem very close to your Uncle Joel?'

'I certainly am.' He paused, and then said, almost to himself. 'He was my father's younger brother. My father died in a motorcycle accident before I was born and it wasn't possible for my mother to look after me alone.'

For an instant it seemed as if a shadow flickered across his face.

'I was brought up by my father's sister, Mary, and her husband, Tom, who treated me like one of their own children. Uncle Joel was there to help in whatever way he could. He helped finance me through university for a start and, because times were hard, paid towards my younger cousin, John's, education too.'

'I take it you've two older brothers,

Matthew and Mark?' she said to lighten his mood.

He laughed. 'No — just a couple more cousins — twins.'

'You're kidding me!'

He shook his head. 'No, their father — my Uncle Tom — is a vicar, so giving everyone biblical names seemed apt. So you see, I've a lot to thank Uncle Joel for and now it's my turn to look out for him.'

She wondered if that last remark was loaded and said stoutly, 'Yes, well, I feel the same way about my aunt. We've had lot of good times up here, and Aunt Mattie and Uncle Ted have been more than generous to all of us.'

'Were they happy together? Your Uncle Ted and Aunt Mattie?'

She looked at him, surprised by the question. Was he wondering what sort of wife her aunt had been? Just in case his uncle was on the verge of popping the question?

'Well, yes, they were a devoted couple. It was a shame he had to work away for so many of their years together but, apart from tourism, it's not easy to find employment up here, you know.'

* * *

When they got back to the guesthouse, she went straight into the kitchen and began to get the supper ready.

She was busy preparing the vegetables when Luke came to join her, found another knife, and started peeling the carrots.

'I'm starving so I thought — if I showed willing — you might ask me to supper as well as Mr Jones,' he said plaintively. 'I could keep the conversation flowing and act as a chaperone.'

'Don't be ridiculous,' she admonished, trying to keep a straight face. 'All right, just this once, but I'm not setting a precedent. I've no intention of providing regular evening meals for you.'

It was a funny sort of evening, mostly spent listening to Mr Jones reminiscing about his days as a civil servant. After coffee, the elderly gentleman smothered a yawn, thanked them both profusely for their hospitality and went up to his room.

'Your aunt and Uncle Joel would be proud of us,' Luke told her.

'I should hope so — and now you can earn your supper and help me with the washing-up!'

He grinned and began to stack the dishes. 'You're a hard taskmaster but I suspect you've got a soft centre!'

'Yes, well, don't push your luck!' she warned him.

'Wouldn't dream of it!' he assured her, and touched her lightly on the arm so that a little frisson trembled along her spine.

Presently, when they went back into the lounge, it was to find Mr Metcalf waiting for them with a special request.

'It's my mother's birthday tomorrow, Lydia, and we wanted to take her out for a meal in the evening, but it's a bit late for the children to stay up and so we were wondering if . . . '

Luke didn't look at Lydia. 'I'm sure we could give them their tea here, then send them up to bed at a reasonable hour and keep an eye on them, couldn't we, Lydia?'

Inwardly amused, she agreed. The Metcalfs were a lovely family who came to visit Ian's mother, who lived near Keswick, several times a year and, because there were too many of them for Mrs Metcalf senior to accommodate, they usually stayed at Hill House.

Ian Metcalf beamed. 'That would be wonderful — and Lydia, we also wanted to ask you if you could do another of your special family portraits — for us to give to my mum as an extra present, before we go home.'

They were still discussing this when Luke excused himself, saying he had some phone calls to make and a few other things to attend to at Willow Cottage.

Lydia finished her discussion with Ian Metcalf and made sure that the other guests, now congregating in the visitors' lounge, were happy.

She made two pots of coffee and a pot of tea for them, just as her aunt would have done and then, feeling rather tired, went off to the private sitting-room to watch TV.

★ ★ ★

Luke did not reappear, and she wondered if one of the phone calls he was making was to a girlfriend or a wife back in London.

After all, he was bound to have a woman in his life, wasn't he? She told herself she was thinking about him far too much considering she'd only known him for a few days.

Her thoughts turned to her relationship with Trent.

Just before she'd come away, he'd asked if he could move in with her and she'd fobbed him off, saying she'd discuss it with him on her return from Silverdale.

Suddenly, she realised that, quite apart from any moral principles she might have, she was against the idea because, deep down, she was uncertain of the strength of her feelings for him. Up until recently, she had thought they had a lot in common, but now she realised that their only mutual interest was their work. She'd enjoyed the exhibitions they'd visited together and found Trent good company, but when she thought about the nightclubs and wine bars he also liked to take her to, she had to admit they weren't really her scene.

And, although Trent had been to her parents' house several times, never once had he taken her to meet his family in Surrey.

True, she had been invited to one or two parties and functions where she had met some of his friends but, if she were honest, she had found them a rather noisy and immature crowd.

There had only been one other man in Lydia's life, before Trent, and he had briefly broken her heart when he had dumped her while she was in her second year at university. After that, apart from the occasional date, she'd mainly just gone about with a group of female friends.

Those friends had eventually all got married or found partners, and she'd felt in danger of being left on the shelf, as her grandmother termed it. Then Trent had entered the studio one day and she'd fallen for him in a big way. Now she wondered if it had just been infatuation on her part.

★ ★ ★

The following day was extraordinarily busy. Three guests left and three more arrived, all with special requirements. One wanted a vegetarian breakfast, another needed a room with shower, not a bath, and the third demanded hot milk at bedtime or she'd never sleep.

Lydia was relieved when Ginny dropped by that afternoon for a chat.

'Jim finished early today so he offered to mind the shop while I came to see how you're getting on.'

They sat over tea and scones in the small garden, soaking up the sunshine.

'You look worn out, Lyddie — when's your sister due to arrive? I think you need a hand.'

'Next Wednesday, but she deserves a break and she'll have Maisie with her.'

'And how are you getting on with Luke, now that he's moved in?'

'Oh, well enough — he's a great hit with the guests — a regular Mr Nice Guy and I have to admit he's proved helpful. This morning the little Metcalf boy up-ended his bowl of porridge all over the floor and Luke cleared it up without a murmur.'

'Well, there you are then — he obviously has his uses. He's always perfectly charming when he comes into the shop, just like his uncle.'

Lydia buttered a scone.

'Well, I can't help thinking he's too good to be true and he seems to have an uncanny knack of popping up just when I'm in the middle of a crisis, and making me feel inadequate. And he always seems to know what's going on before he's even been told. No, I'm afraid I still can't fathom his motives for being here.'

The elderly sisters from room five came into the garden at that moment. One of them was clutching her jaw.

'I've lost a filling. Is there a dentist round here, my dear?'

'I told you you oughtn't to eat toffees, Phyllis,' her sister scolded.

'I'm afraid you'll have to go into Keswick, Miss Timms,' Lydia informed her, and took the old lady off to the office so that she could use the telephone to arrange an appointment . . .

Miss Timms eventually put down the receiver, looking dejected.

'They said they can fit me in as an emergency if I can get into Keswick by five o'clock, but there isn't a bus — is there a taxi?'

'What's the problem?' Luke asked, appearing in the doorway, and when Miss Timms told him what had happened, he immediately offered to run her into Keswick himself.

As they settled back in the garden, Ginny said, 'What did I tell you, Lydia? He's absolutely charming.'

But Lydia wasn't convinced. 'Hmm. Strange how he's always there to help in an emergency. I'm beginning to think he's trying to prove a point — that I can't cope on my own!'

'Now you're being paranoid! You should be grateful he's here to help out.' Ginny leaned back in her chair. 'Now, changing the subject, you still haven't told me about you and Trent. The other day you mentioned you had a few issues . . . '

Lydia was still thinking about Luke and came to with a start.

'He was just a bit peeved that I was going to be away for a while, that's all.'

Ginny gazed at her friend. 'Really? I suspect there's more to it than that.

How long have I known you? Come on — you can tell me.'

Lydia had never been able to keep secrets from Ginny.

'The thing is, Trent wants us to move in together.'

'Wow, well that's pretty good, isn't it?' Ginny studied her. 'No, judging by your expression, apparently not. I thought you were mad about him — so what's the problem?'

Lydia fingered her bracelet. It was rather heavy and jangly and not really to her taste, but it had been a present from Trent, so she wore it from time to time.

'Oh, I don't know — call me old-fashioned if you like but . . .'

Ginny propped her elbows on the table and surveyed her thoughtfully.

'You think Trent isn't ready for commitment and just wants you to be there for him,' she prompted. 'Without all the responsibilities that go with marriage?'

Lydia nodded. 'That's it exactly. I couldn't have put it better myself. But we have a business partnership, too, remember — so, if I refuse, it's going to be awkward facing him each day.'

'I don't see why it should be,' Ginny told her. 'Just because you don't want him to move in with you, it doesn't mean you can't continue to have a relationship. Of course, if you don't care about him romantically any more, then things could be a bit awkward, but not impossible, surely?'

Lydia threw some crumbs to a hopeful sparrow.

'Another thing — my flat is rather cramped. I like my own space and I'm not sure if I want to give up my independence quite yet.'

'What I think you really mean is that you're not sure if you really love him, because if you did then you wouldn't hesitate — or is it that you don't think he truly loves you?'

Lydia considered. 'If our feelings for each other were deep enough then, surely, marriage would be the only way . . . ?'

'Well, nowadays, there are plenty of folk with long-term relationships who seem perfectly happy not to marry,' Ginny pointed out.

'Yes, I know, but it isn't right for everyone, surely? You see, I think Trent would be moving in for all the wrong reasons. He's sharing a flat with a couple of other guys at the moment and I know he doesn't like it. I'm afraid he'd just see me as someone to do his washing and ironing, to cook his meals and darn his socks.'

Ginny hooted with laughter. 'No-one darns socks nowadays!'

'Well, you know what I mean!'

'Lazy is he, this Trent? From what you've told me, it sounds as if you'd be better off without him. Anyway, you've got plenty of time to think about things while you're up here. Have you heard from Mattie and Joel yet?'

'Luke's had one or two text messages and e-mails from Joel, but Aunt Mattie doesn't like technology, so I guess I'll have to wait for a postcard. But from what Joel's told Luke, they appear to be having a great time.'

'Good for them. So why don't you look very happy about it? I realise that both yourself and Luke have got the welfare of two lovely people at heart and want to ensure that they aren't making the biggest mistake of their lives by getting romantically involved, and I think that's very commendable, Lyddie, but I'm not sure either of them would thank you for interfering!'

'I'm not,' Lydia protested fiercely, 'but I think Luke is. He seems overly keen to keep an eye on what's going on here. He seems to be acquainting himself with all sorts of aspects of Aunt Mattie's business.'

'Well, if Joel is is thinking of joining forces with your aunt then perhaps he's asked Luke to give him a professional opinion on how Hill House is being managed. After all, didn't you tell me he's in the hotel business?'

'Yes, that's what worries me. What

sort of plans might he have for this place?'

Ginny raised her eyes skywards. 'Lydia, I've told you before, you're reading far too much into the situation. What harm can it possibly do if he comes up with a few suggestions for improvements? Let's face it, this is a lovely old house, but it is a tad shabby and, as it stands, could never attract the sort of clientele who were prepared to pay more than a very basic rate!'

'But that's the way Aunt Mattie likes it, don't you see? The people she wants to stay here are those who enjoy the beauty of the Lakes, but who haven't got particularly deep pockets. They have clean and comfortable rooms, a hearty breakfast and are made to feel welcome. The very fact that they return year upon year speaks for itself, doesn't it?'

When Ginny had gone, Lydia cleared away the tea things and sorted out a pile of laundry. She realised that, although their chat had helped, she was still feeling uneasy about a number of things and, for the moment, Luke Carstairs remained at the top of the list.

A Day Out

Luke returned with a very grateful Miss Timms who declared her intention to go and have a little lie down.

'Thanks for that,' Lydia told him. 'Good thing you were around,' she added reluctantly.

He grinned, 'Well, taking elderly ladies to the dentist will look good on my CV, I reckon. Now, how d'you fancy fish and chips for supper?'

'What a brilliant idea — with mushy peas, of course, but it's quite a long drive to the nearest chippy so it might be quicker if I went, since I know all the short cuts. You can hold the fort!'

By the time she returned with the food, he had put some plates to warm, laid the table and cut some bread, and was making a dressing for a side salad.

'Your sister rang while you were out

— asked you to call her back,' he told her.

'Thanks — I expect it's regarding next week. Don't know if I've mentioned it, but she's bringing her little girl up for a few days over the half-term holiday. Jenny's husband, Colin, works away and so she's on her own with Maisie a lot of the time. I'll ring her back after we've eaten.'

* * *

To her surprise, she enjoyed the meal, which Luke insisted on paying for. He was a pleasant companion, but she realised again that, while he was good at getting information from her, he wasn't too keen to talk about himself.

'So tell me a bit more about your work,' he said, reaching for the vinegar. 'What sort of photography does your business partner do?'

She didn't want to discuss Trent and said airily, 'Oh, weddings, passport photos, models' portfolios — school photo sessions — that sort of thing.'

'Sounds interesting, but if you're self-employed you must be losing quite a bit of work while you're up here.'

'Well, I'd be due time off anyway, and whenever I'm up here in Silverdale, I generally get a few commissions from local hotels. That's how I started off, you know, taking photographs of the guests whenever I've been staying up here, either on holiday or helping out Aunt Mattie. I've got a friend in Keswick who used to share my studio with me in Kent. We have a sort of loose arrangement. Whenever I'm up here, I take on one or two of her hotel assignments and she lets me use her studio to develop and mount any special photos that I need to get ready — like the one for the Metcalfs.'

To her surprise, he suddenly looked disapproving. 'I see, and when you're off doing all this, who exactly will be left in charge here?'

'Oh, you don't need to concern yourself on that score,' she said defensively. 'As I've told you before, our guests always have a contact number in case of an emergency.'

His eyes narrowed. 'And supposing someone is taken ill or has an accident and you're on the other side of the lake?'

'Not being medically qualified, I wouldn't be much use anyway, but there's a doctor in the village, and his district nurse lives near here too. Anyway, why are you so bothered? It's hardly your concern.'

He helped himself to more salad. 'That's where you're mistaken. I've told you the nature of my job and, as my uncle's thinking of investing in Hill House, then I'm sure he'd welcome my input and advice.'

She gaped at him. 'Aunt Mattie owns this house — it's her home! Why on earth would she need anyone to invest in it?'

He looked around him with a critical air and she had to admit that, as Ginny had tactfully pointed out, the place was looking a bit shabby and in need of refurbishment. It was a large, rambling old house that had had a fair amount of wear and tear in recent years with guests traipsing through it.

Aunt Mattie, bless her, never really noticed things like faded carpets, curtains or wallpaper, but obviously others did.

'This place has a lot of potential, but it needs a lot doing to it,' he said, stating the obvious.

'Well, if it doesn't suit you, you can always go back to your swish London hotel. Aunt Mattie hasn't asked for your opinion,' she said with a spark of anger. 'I expect she'll get around to some decorating during the winter months.'

'It's scheduled for the autumn, I believe, when the seasonal rush has died down,' he informed her in his usual unruffled manner, 'together with some alterations — a couple more en suites and some modernisation to the communal bathrooms for starters.'

She couldn't believe her ears. 'How

come you know so much about everything?' she demanded. 'Anyone would think Aunt Mattie was employing you as a consultant.'

A slight smile played about his lips. 'No, but Uncle Joel asked my advice and I gave it — that's all. Don't open your mouth like that — you look like a goldfish!'

She gasped, the colour suffusing her cheeks. The man was insufferable — an infuriating busybody. Just when she was beginning to like him, he was showing himself in his true colours! She swept up the plates, left them in a bowl of soapy water and went off to phone her sister, Jenny, her head reeling.

* * *

Jenny sounded fraught. 'Thank goodness you've rung back, Lydia. I'm afraid I've got bad news. Colin's mum's had a minor accident — hurt her ankle. Nothing too serious, but I'm afraid I'll have to postpone coming up for at least a few days. Anyway, listen — Nell's got some holiday due, so she's volunteered to bring Maisie to Silverdale.'

Lydia groaned inwardly as she thought of Jenny's young sister-in-law.

'But Nell's not used to children — you've said so yourself.'

'Yes, well, she's been faced with the choice of either taking Maisie to the Lakes or staying here for her entire holiday to look after Marcia, so she's decided on a compromise. She'll spend a few days with her mother, to give me a chance to get things organised here, and then she'll come on up to you.'

'Maisie I can cope with, but not Nell!' Lydia protested.

Jenny laughed. 'Oh, I promise it'll only be for a short while. I'll join you just as soon as Marcia's able to manage on her own again.'

The temporary job which Lydia had thought would be so straightforward was fast turning into a nightmare. 'I suppose Nell must be footloose and fancy free again if she's willing to give up her free time for the sake of someone other than herself?'

'How did you guess? She's just finished with her latest boyfriend. Anyway, she'll be arriving with Maisie on Wednesday afternoon. Now, how's this mysterious lodger of yours?'

Lydia brought her sister up to date with all that had been happening, including what Luke had just said about the refurbishment.

Jenny whistled. 'Well, Hill House could certainly do with a makeover.'

'But, surely — if Joel puts up the money — then he'll be able to claim it back if things don't work out. What's his motive?'

'I'd have thought that was pretty obvious! It's because his relationship with Aunt Mattie has become serious. Look, I think the best thing you can do is to keep things running smoothly until she returns and then see if you can get her to tell you what her plans are. But, although it sounds to me as if you're managing perfectly well without my help, being your older sister, I'll be happier once I can get myself up there to check out this man of mystery.'

Lydia grunted. 'He's one of those characters who seem to have the gift of getting along with everyone on the surface, but I suspect there's another side to him.'

'There's another side to most people. Did you say he's got three brothers?'

'Cousins — his father died before he was born and he was brought up by Joel's sister and her husband.' A thought suddenly struck her. 'Just imagine if they all came up here!'

Jenny laughed. 'We'll cross that bridge when we come to it. Anyway, I'll keep in touch but, don't forget, I'll be at my mum-in-law's during the day-time, from Wednesday onwards.'

* * *

Luke was doing the washing-up when she returned to the kitchen. He had tied Mrs Dalton's frilly apron round his waist and she wanted to laugh because it looked so comical, but she was still too cross with him to relax in his company.

'My sister's mother-in-law's had an accident and so Jenny doesn't feel she can leave her to come up here.'

Luke looked sympathetic. 'Tough luck.'

'Yes, it is, and my little niece was really disappointed, so Jenny's arranged for her sister-in-law to bring her up next Wednesday. I'm not sure how that's going to work out because Nell's not good with children.'

'Right — then we'll have to do the best we can to see that the kid's kept entertained.'

He began drying the dishes and Lydia put them away.

'I'm popping into Keswick tomorrow, to meet up with the friend who's got the photographic studio so, while I'm there, I'll see if I can pick up a few things to keep Maisie amused.'

'D'you know I might just come with

you. I'd like to see a bit more of Keswick than just the inside of a dental surgery.'

'But I thought you were concerned that one of us needed to be here in case of any problems?'

He shrugged. 'Yes, well, you've managed to convince me that you've got sufficient back-up in place and, as you've pointed out, most of the guests are usually out until late afternoon anyway . . . Shall we take my car?'

She found herself agreeing, almost without meaning to. What was it with this man? It was as if he could charm the birds off the trees.

* * *

It was a glorious drive to Keswick the following morning. Lydia never failed to be stirred by the beauty of the landscape. The fells towered majestically in the background, the sun striking them with gold.

Luke drove in silence for a few miles

66

and Lydia, acutely aware of his presence, found herself stealing glances at him. Although he wasn't handsome in a conventional sort of way, his rugged looks and expressive brown eyes made him decidedly attractive. His hair fell forward across his brow, softening his strong features. She wondered if Joel had looked anything like Luke when he was younger.

★ ★ ★

The market town of Keswick was buzzing with tourists.

She showed Luke where to park and when he made to go off said, 'Come and meet Anthea. She'll never forgive me if I don't introduce you. She knows Aunt Mattie and has met Joel a couple of times.'

Anthea Fenwick was a plump, attractive young woman with a distinctly bohemian look. She wore a loose-fitting, Indian cotton dress and had tied a colourful bandana around her mass of untidy red hair. She greeted Lydia with a hug and shook Luke's hand enthusiastically, chatting away to him as if she'd known him all her life, managing to extract more information from him in half an hour than Lydia had done during the entire time he'd been at Hill House.

She gave him a tour of her studio, and he admired the selection of photographs showing people as they went about their daily work in Cumbria, that adorned the buttercup yellow walls.

'There's an exhibition coming up in July and I thought I'd submit some entries for the leisure and landscape sections. People are very into photography these days. It's the new art form — has Lydia shown you any of her work?'

Luke was studying some scenes of Derwentwater through the seasons and looked up with a smile. 'I've only seen the photographs that are hanging on the walls at Hill House but, judging from those, she's obviously very talented.'

'She certainly is — her animal studies are really special. I'm hoping you'll put one or two of them into the exhibition, Lyddie.'

'I'll think about it,' Lydia assured her, feeling a glow of pleasure at Luke's unexpected compliment.

'So, what do you do in your spare time, Luke? Are you an outdoor person?' Anthea asked as they sat down to coffee and cake.

'Well, as I live in London, I take every opportunity to escape to the countryside on my days off. I enjoy walking but, other than that, I like to cook.'

Lydia looked at him in disbelief. 'That explains the take-away fish and chips we had last night!'

Anthea winked at Luke. 'Our Lydia's got a bit of an acid tongue at times, but her bark is worse than her bite.'

'So I assume that, if you're in hotel management, Luke, you started off doing a spell in the kitchen?' Anthea asked him.

'Yes, spot on. And I find cooking relaxing. But Lydia is quite capable in the kitchen — so why not let someone else do it, while I've got the opportunity?' He got to his feet. 'Talking of food, Lydia, I'll see you for lunch around one-thirty.'

He gave Anthea a captivating smile.

'Delighted to meet you, Anthea. Thanks for coffee and you're more than welcome to join us for lunch?'

She returned his smile. 'Sadly, I've appointments from two o'clock onwards, so another time?'

As the door closed behind him she said, 'He's gorgeous, Lyddie. Oh, not so devastatingly good-looking as Trent, of course, but with Trent it's only skin deep. This one's got style.'

'Do you think so?'

'Oh, yes. Charm, such a lovely smile, and those dark eyes, and as for that muscular frame! Yes, I'd award him eight out of ten.'

Lydia laughed, inwardly agreeing with every word. 'Whatever would Mike say if he heard you?'

'He'd know there's absolutely no contest. He's pretty safe there! Doesn't stop me admiring a nice-looking guy though, does it? Now, I'd like to know a bit more about the inner man. What makes Luke Carstairs tick?'

'Well, that's my problem,' Lydia told her. 'Everyone says how charming he is and I don't deny he can be, but there's something I'm still not sure about . . . call it intuition on my part. I can't help feeling that he's here for reasons other than giving advice about redecorating. The thing is, he seems so keen to protect Joel's interests, but I can't understand why. After all, Joel's just got Willow Cottage, whereas my aunt's got by far the bigger property with the most potential, and she is quite a wealthy widow.'

Anthea collected up the mugs. 'You're sure about that are you

— about your aunt being well off?' she asked casually.

Lydia picked up the empty plates. 'Well, Uncle Ted certainly left her well provided for, and he also left money to my parents and the three of us, too. As you know, I put mine into my studio.'

Anthea looked thoughtful. 'Hmm. Has it actually occurred to you that Luke might not be so much protecting his uncle's interests as preserving his own? After all, if he's Joel's nephew then perhaps he would stand to inherit something if anything happens to Joel — I mean Joel is a bachelor, isn't he?'

Lydia stared at her friend. 'Yes, but, as I've just said, he's probably not that well off.'

Anthea was renowned for her direct speech. 'How on earth would you know that? Look, let's be realistic, Lyddie. Have you got any idea of the price of property up here nowadays? I bet Joel had to pay an arm and a leg for Willow Cottage, and he's having it done up and is also obviously prepared to help out with refurbishing Hill House.'

Lydia bit her lip. 'Put like that, things seem even more complicated than I'd previously thought.'

'If you want my opinion, I'd leave well alone,' Anthea told her. 'Now, changing the subject, tell me about you and Trent.'

'Oh, he's fine. A bit fed up that I'm up here, but he's got plenty of work to keep him out of mischief . . . now, can we run over those hotel bookings for next week?'

She got out her filofax and, suddenly, the two of them became businesslike.

★ ★ ★

For lunch, Luke took her to a charming restaurant overlooking Lake Derwentwater. 'Ginny recommended it,' he told her, catching her surprised look.

It was warm enough to sit on the terrace and she sighed with pleasure.

They had trout with fresh vegetables, followed by crème brûlée and coffee.

During the meal, Luke told her that, after he'd left her at Anthea's studio, he'd paid a visit to the Cumberland Pencil Museum.

He watched her visibly relaxing as she recounted how her Uncle Ted had taken her brother, sister and herself to the museum when they were children. Her brother had dropped his brand-new pencil down a drain almost as soon as they'd got outside.

After that, they exchanged one or two more anecdotes about their respective childhoods, Luke telling her a bit about his upbringing as part of a large family in Surrey. He obviously got on well with his aunt and uncle and his cousins, and she felt she had made a bit of progress towards getting to know him.

As they sat over their coffee, he said casually, 'So what about you? It must have been a wrench leaving Yorkshire to go down south. Do you ever go back?'

'Occasionally, although our only connection with Yorkshire these days is Aunt Mattie's sister, Janet. She and

Mattie have always made my family very welcome.'

There was a curious expression on Luke's face. 'So, do you still visit her?'

'Well, I haven't been to see her for a couple of years, but we keep in touch. My parents called to see her last year when they rented a cottage in the area.'

'And does she ever come to stay at Hill House?'

'Now and again. In fact, I'm sure Aunt Mattie said she'd be visiting at the end of the season when Hill House closes for the winter.'

She wondered why Luke was so interested, and then realised that Janet was probably the closest relation Mattie had. Was he trying to establish who else, other than Lydia's family, might have an interest in Mattie's affairs?

'What's with all the questions? If you want to know whether Aunt Mattie has any more relations then — so far as I'm aware — no, she hasn't,' she informed him, watching closely for his reaction.

There was a determined tilt to his

chin. 'She could have twenty cousins living in Timbuktu for all I care. I was just making polite conversation!' he said sharply.

She was surprised by his tone and was now more convinced than ever that he was intent on discovering all he could about her aunt, and was even more certain that it must have something to do with his disapproval of Joel's relationship with her.

Lydia helped herself to another chocolate-covered disc of Kendal mint cake and decided it was time to change the subject.

'What are you planning to do this afternoon?' she asked him. 'I'll need to put in another hour at Anthea's studio, preparing the print of the family group for Mr Metcalf's mother's birthday, but I don't need to start right this very minute.'

He leaned back in his chair and consulted his watch. 'How about we do something together for an hour or so and then go our separate ways for the rest of the afternoon? Got any ideas?'

'Yes,' she told him, suddenly deciding exactly what they could do. 'Come on — that was a lovely meal, but now I feel the need for some exercise.'

She took him to the launch pier where, despite his protests, she hired a rowing boat.

'Trust me — I'm quite good at this. Uncle Ted used to take us on the lake when we were small and I've been on a couple of outdoor pursuits courses.'

'Well, I'm warning you, I've never rowed in my life before, so I'm entirely in your hands — help!' And he pulled a comical face so that she couldn't help laughing.

After a short while under her expert tuition, he proved to be quite competent with the oars.

The afternoon sun made the water sparkle like so many jewels and she pointed out all the landmarks. 'That's St Herbert's Island and then there's Derwent Island and over there is Friar's Crag — a popular beauty spot.' She sighed. 'It's all so lovely, isn't it!'

He looked at her animated expression. Her cheeks were tinged with pink and her hair was escaping from the slide she'd secured it with.

'Do you think you might come to live here permanently some day?'

She looked thoughtful. 'I don't know. Part of me is here and always will be and I consider myself fortunate to be able to visit Aunt Mattie two or three times a year, but it's not that easy to find work up here and mine is a specialist field.'

* * *

Later, as they walked back into the town, Lydia realised how much she'd enjoyed his company. Suddenly he stopped and took her hands between his and she lowered her gaze, afraid that she might give herself away.

'I've thoroughly enjoyed today,' he said, and stooping, he kissed her cheek before walking away.

As she made her way back to Anthea's studio, Lydia realised that her heart was beating a wild tattoo. Luke was certainly a charmer and she realised that she was in danger of falling under his spell. Well, it would not do, she told herself firmly. He was still very much an unknown quantity and she couldn't be doing with any more complications in her life. She tried to conjure up an image of Trent in her mind's eye and failed, seeing Luke each time.

For the rest of that afternoon, she found it so difficult to concentrate on what she was doing that, when Luke came to fetch her, she'd managed to put the finishing touches to the Metcalfs' photograph but hadn't completed her other tasks, and arranged to call on Anthea again in a couple of days' time.

★ ★ ★

When they returned to Hill House, it was to find that the youngest Metcalf child was proudly sporting a butterfly stitch having fallen off a climbing frame, and that there was a young couple hovering by the reception desk, hoping to book-in.

As it happened, there was a vacancy but as soon as Lydia came back downstairs after showing the couple to their twin room, Luke said, 'They look a bit suspicious to me. And very young. The girl didn't look much more than seventeen. I wouldn't be surprised if they've run away from home.'

Lydia groaned. 'I did wonder, but the girl's wearing a wedding ring.'

'Don't let that fool you, it probably belonged to her grandmother!' He indicated the guest book. 'Have you seen what they've written in here?'

She peered over his shoulder. 'Donna and Dale Main — so what's wrong with that?'

He picked up a leaflet from the desk advertising Dalemain, a stately home in the vicinity, and she coloured for not being more observant.

'Do you think we should to contact the authorities in case they're on the run?' Lydia asked Luke.

He considered. 'No — let's leave it for tonight. We'll hear soon enough if there's a problem.'

Presently, the young couple came back downstairs, wondering if they could get something to eat. 'Anything would do,' said the girl.

Here we go again, thought Lydia, just as Luke stepped in. 'Jacket potatoes and baked beans do you?'

The young couple wolfed down the food as if they hadn't eaten for a week and went back to their room shortly afterwards.

★ ★ ★

It was at about half-past five the following morning that Lydia awoke feeling that things weren't right. Slipping on a dressinggown she crept down to the kitchen to discover Luke making tea. He reached for another mug and pulled out a chair.

'Our love birds have flown the nest and weren't particularly quiet about it. I had my window open and one of them tripped over the milk bottles. I just saw them slipping away down the lane — no hope of catching them.'

The full impact of what he was saying hit her. 'They left without paying the bill!'

He shrugged. 'I doubt if they had two halfpennies to rub together, anyway. But they'll get caught sooner or later.'

'But shouldn't we phone the police?'

He poured the tea. 'Oh, I've done that already. What are you grinning at?'

'I was just thinking you're looking very dashing in that outfit — straight out of a Noel Coward play!'

Luke was attired in a silky, maroon dressing-gown. He chuckled.

'Oh, I borrowed it from Uncle Joel. You're looking quite delightful yourself, if I'm allowed to say so.'

She yawned and pushed her hair off her face. 'It's too early for chat up lines, don't you think? I'm impervious. I could do with a bit more shut-eye, but I don't suppose there's any chance of that.'

'Well, I could always cook breakfast,' he volunteered, 'so that you can have a bit of a lie-in?'

She sighed. 'Much as I'm tempted, I can't accept — I'm expecting a couple of new guests around mid-morning after Phyllis Timms and her sister have left.'

'What a pity — tell you what; I'll still cook breakfast — give you a breathing space.'

He reached out and touched her cheek. 'That thing you're wearing suits you and your hair is lovely loose like that.'

'It gets in the way,' she told him and pushed it back, her heart racing. What was it about this man? He had the power to set her emotions in turmoil and yet she'd only known him for five minutes. Perhaps Joel Norris had the same effect on Aunt Mattie?

She pulled herself together with an effort and, finishing her tea said, 'Thanks, I'm wide awake now so I might as well get dressed. By all means do breakfast if you like — it'll give me an opportunity to catch up on some paperwork in the office.'

★ ★ ★

Presently, the police rang. The young runaways, who had both turned out to be sixteen, had been reported missing by their respective families and had been apprehended on board a train bound for Scotland.

'They left an IOU in their room and a five pound note,' Lydia told Luke with a grin.

'Love's sweet dream, eh? Let's hope they don't get separated by their irate parents when they arrive back home — it seems they've hitched from Yorkshire. What it is to be that age, with all your life stretching before you, and so deeply in love!'

She stared at him, surprised by his sentiments. 'I thought you'd be disapproving!'

There was a faraway look in his eyes. 'My parents weren't much older than those two — they had dreams too — dreams that were sadly shattered. Those two young things deserve a chance before life touches them and turns them cynical.'

'You sound as if you're speaking from the heart — are you cynical?'

He shook his head. 'No, not really, but I know plenty of people who are — now tell me, have you managed to catch up with the paperwork?'

'More or less — Aunt Mattie usually gets me to take a look at the books while I'm here.'

'Would you like me to . . .'

She gave him a sharp look. 'Not without her permission — no way!'

He held up his hands, surprised at her reaction. 'Whoa — I was only offering to help. I wouldn't dream of being a sticky beak.'

She pulled herself together. Perhaps he genuinely did want to help. After all, he must have a fair amount of expertise. She gave a little laugh.

'Well, if you really want to help, I'll tell you what you can do. You've set a precedent,' she told him. 'The Metcalf children loved the pancakes you made this morning and asked if they could have them for their breakfast again tomorrow. I'm no good with pancakes and it's Mrs Dalton's day off, so it looks as if you've got yourself a regular slot.'

* * *

That evening, Luke agreed to hold the fort while Lydia took over one of Anthea's commissions. She always enjoyed them. The guests in the local hotel were very amiable and happy for her to photograph them, and she was glad of the opportunity to renew her acquaintance with the staff.

She did the usual round of tables,

which were a mixture of young and old folk, and then, after she had handed out some of Anthea's business cards, there were a few requests for special photographs — for birthdays, anniversaries etc. — which she would arrange to have taken by her friend.

She was invited to stay on and have a drink in the bar, and it was quite late before she arrived back at Hill House, to find Luke still up, thumbing through a magazine in Aunt Mattie's sitting-room.

He looked up and gave her one of his smiles.

'Was it a good evening?'

She nodded, her heart doing strange things.

She told him about her evening.

'So, how many more of these commissions do you have?'

'Oh, only another two or three. It gives Anthea a break to go out with her husband and she knows I enjoy doing them. In fact, one of the hotels is giving her space for an exhibition later in the year and they've invited me to show some of my work, too.'

'Hmm, any chance of my coming with you on one of your appointments? One night when your sister's here, perhaps?'

She stared at him in surprise, her heart missing a beat. 'Well, I imagine so. I'm sure they wouldn't mind if I told them I was bringing a friend — particularly as you're in the hotel business.'

He frowned. 'I'd rather you didn't mention that. Actually, I'd be interested to see the inside of one or two hotels round here, but I wouldn't like them to think I was visiting in a rival capacity.'

She swallowed, feeling an overwhelming sense of disappointment. Of course, that was it! How could she have been so naïve as to think that Luke wanted to come with her because he enjoyed her company?

It was evident that he was a business man through and through and only wanted to compare notes and pick up ideas for projects of his own.

She told herself she was foolish to care. After all, she had a boyfriend waiting for her back in Kent, and she had no intention of two-timing him.

A Decision For Lydia

On Sunday after breakfast, Luke declared his intention of going for a walk and asked Lydia if she'd like to join him. 'After church, of course — I gather we've just got time to make it to the morning service.'

She smiled at him. 'I'm glad to see your clergyman uncle hasn't put you off.'

'For your information, I used to be a choir boy, and one of my cousins is a curate,' he said, looking amused.

Mr Jones and three elderly lady guests accompanied them to church but, while the others stayed behind for coffee, Luke and Lydia slipped away and went back to Hill House to prepare a picnic and collect their backpacks.

They decided to go to Dovedale Beck, near Patterdale, and set off in Lydia's car this time, as it was smaller and easier to manoeuvre than Luke's.

When they arrived at Cow Bridge, they were fortunate enough to find a parking space, and headed off on a gentle, relaxing walk along wooded paths, from where they caught glimpses of Brothers Water.

Presently, emerging from the valley, they followed the beck until they came to a quiet picnic spot. Luke sank down on to the grass and looked around him at the glorious scenery.

'How come I've missed all this for so long?' he asked.

'It's a well-kept secret amongst the hundreds that come here each year,' she teased.

After a picnic of rolls, fruit and pieces of Kendal mint cake washed down by coffee, they went on their way again.

'This is bliss — the air's like wine,' he commented and, before she realised it, he had caught her hand in his and swung her round to face him.

'Thanks for coming with me and showing me all this, Lydia. I'd like to think we could be friends from now on. Our paths are bound to cross from time to time if my uncle and your aunt are going to be running Hill House together.'

She caught her breath. His smile was captivating and there was a gleam in his brown eyes as they locked with her own blue-grey ones.

'I'm willing to give it a go,' she said unsteadily, aware that there was an undeniable attraction between them and wondering if he sensed it too.

The view was breathtaking and she felt invigorated as they walked back alongside the beck.

'Helps to put everything in perspective, doesn't it? I can understand how the poets were inspired — Wordsworth, Coleridge and Southey.'

'Stand still,' she commanded.

He looked surprised but, obediently, did as he was bid, and she photographed him.

He grinned. 'I've probably broken the camera. How about letting me take one of you — don't worry, I'll use my own camera!'

During the drive back to Silverdale, he said, 'So your little niece is coming on Wednesday with her other aunt?'

'Yes — Maisie's eight and quite a live wire. She and Jodie Metcalf are great friends, which is really why Jenny's letting her come with Nell, otherwise she would have missed her chum because the Metcalfs are going home next week.'

'So what about Nell?' he asked casually.

'Oh, she works in London and will probably be bored within a day or two, but apparently she's got some university friends who live nearby, so she'll be able to visit them.'

Nell was a restless individual. She was also extremely attractive and fond of a good time. As the youngest child in her family, she had been over-indulged by her doting parents and was so used to having her own way that she was inclined to make life difficult for anyone who attempted to thwart her. She had never been to Hill House before and Lydia wondered how she'd cope in such a rural location.

★ ★ ★

It rained solidly for the next twenty-four hours and several of the guests opted to stay put for much of the day which meant that Lydia felt obliged to offer soup, sandwiches and hot drinks at lunch time — for such a reasonable rate that she barely covered the costs.

Luke lent a hand before going off to Willow Cottage for a while, saying he had things there to attend to.

Then Nell and Maisie arrived as promised in the middle of Wednesday afternoon.

Maisie, hot, sticky and overtired, scrambled out of the car to fling herself at Lydia, complaining that she was thirsty.

Luke greeted the child cheerfully but Maisie was cautious and stood beside

Lydia, staring at him.

Nell herself climbed elegantly out of the car — a stunning blonde with large, cornflower-blue eyes and a slender figure.

Luke took her small hand in his and she smiled up at him, fluttering her absurdly long lashes. She always managed to bring out the protective instinct in men. She looked like a delicate Dresden figurine thought Lydia, although, in actual fact, Nell was quite capable of taking care of herself.

'Come on in. You must be exhausted after such a long drive. I'll get your luggage,' Luke told her.

'Just Maisie's, thanks. I've arranged to stay with friends near Keswick.'

Lydia was taken aback. 'But I thought you were staying here to look after Maisie!'

'Trudi and Rob — my friends from university days — are up here house-sitting for Rob's mother while she's on holiday, and they've invited me to stay with them. Surely it makes sense? After all, it'll free an extra room here.'

'Well, no, it won't actually. You were to have had the twin-bedded room that Jenny would have shared with Maisie — at least for the time being.'

Nell looked positively aghast. 'Oh, but I couldn't possibly share a room with anyone! I like my privacy.'

'But the whole point of you being here was for you to stay and help with Maisie! You know I've got my hands full — especially first thing in the morning,' Lydia said, inwardly seething.

Nell's cheeks were slightly pink. 'Oh, come on. I've only got a couple of weeks' holiday and I've already been at home for several days, looking after Mother.'

Maisie's lip trembled. 'Perhaps I could live with you and Rob and Trudi?' she suggested to Nell.

Nell patted her head. 'Sorry, angel. Rob doesn't really like kids. Besides, your little friends are staying here, aren't they?'

Maisie nodded, brightening as she

remembered the Metcalfs. 'But I can come and visit you at Rob and Trudi's can't I? You promised I could!' She turned to Lydia. 'Rob's mum's got a juicy and a swimming pool. Aunty Nell says she'll ask him if I can use the juicy.'

Lydia and Luke exchanged puzzled glances and then Luke said, with a sudden flash of inspiration, 'Well, we've got a machine here that makes smoothies — at least my Uncle Joel has and I'm sure he won't mind if we borrow it.'

Maisie stared at him blankly and Nell gave a trill of laughter.

'She means a jacuzzi — not a juicer! I haven't actually asked Rob yet, but I'm sure it'll be OK for you all to come over one evening for drinks. I'll give you a ring.'

'Well, I'm afraid we're no competition for Rob's house,' Luke said. 'We don't have a swimming pool or a juicy.'

Nell gave another tinkling little laugh, and then smiled at Maisie.

'Be a good girl, poppet, and I'll take you shopping like I promised. We'll buy something special for you to wear.'

'Aren't you even staying for supper?' Lydia asked incredulously.

'No. Rob and Trudi are expecting me. I wouldn't mind a coffee, though.'

They sat out on the small terrace with their drinks and Maisie wandered off to play in the garden.

'Lydia tells me you work in London, Nell. Whereabouts?' asked Luke.

The two of them chattered away as if they had known each other for years.

Watching them, Lydia was aware of a sudden inexplicable pang of envy. In spite of the long journey, Nell still managed to look glamorous. She was wearing a low-necked green top with black trousers, and long, dangly jade earrings. Lydia suddenly felt decidedly out of it and, getting up, went across to chat to her little niece.

★ ★ ★

After Nell had departed, Maisie looked a bit lost but, surprisingly, Luke came to the rescue and took her off to show her the dolls' house he'd found tucked away at the back of the cupboard in his room, and which he was cleaning up for small guests to enjoy.

She was delighted to be reunited with the Metcalf children, who put in an appearance shortly afterwards, and she went outside to play with them.

It wasn't long before she came rushing back in.

'Mr Metcalf is taking Jodie and the others to the field to play rounders. Can I go with them?'

'Well, just so long as you're back for your tea at six.'

'Tell you what, Lydia,' Luke volunteered, 'why don't I cook tea so that you can go and play rounders with Maisie?'

'Great — I'll go and get my trainers,' shouted Maisie as she rushed away up the stairs.

Lydia had a carefree time with the

children. Young Maisie was good at rounders and, after a hectic game, they left the Metcalfs having a picnic tea in the field and went back into the house.

Interesting smells were coming from the kitchen and Lydia sent her niece upstairs to wash and brush up and went to investigate. Luke was stirring something in a saucepan.

'Spaghetti bolognese OK with you?' he asked her.

'Sounds — and smells — good to me. But I'd better go and freshen up, too, before we sit down to eat. It's a while since I've done anything quite so energetic — I think I'm out of condition.'

He surveyed her, and thought she looked positively delightful. Her hair was escaping from her scrunchie and strands fell about her face. Her blue-grey eyes sparkled and there was a smudge of dirt on one cheek. He knew it would be all too easy to get involved with this young woman . . .

With a great effort, he pulled himself together just as Maisie reappeared, fair hair flying about her shoulders.

'Jodie's mum says I can go out with them tomorrow — they're going to Trotters World Of Animals . . . Is that OK?' She looked at Lydia with eager blue eyes.

'I'm sure it will be, but perhaps we ought to check with your mum when we phone her this evening?'

★   ★   ★

Tea was a great success. Maisie told Luke that his spaghetti bolognese was almost as good as her mum's!

He laughed and ruffled her hair.

'That's praise indeed!' said Lydia.

After they'd eaten, she and Maisie went to have a chat with Jenny on the phone and Lydia mentioned the Metcalfs' invitation.

'Yes, that's fine. I know how well all the children get on. I only wish I could be with you, but Colin's mother really can't manage on her own, not quite yet.'

'Don't worry, Jen. I'm coping fine,' Lydia assured her, 'although I have to admit it was a bit of a shock to discover Nell wasn't staying here to look after Maisie.'

There was an audible gasp from the other end of the phone.

'What? Just wait till I get hold of that young madam! I suppose she's staying with those friends of hers. She hasn't breathed a word about this to me! Well, it's just not good enough!'

'Not to worry. Luke's proving to be amazingly good with children and he cooks like a dream — he made the tea tonight. I still can't weigh him up, though.'

★ ★ ★

Lydia encountered another problem when Maisie told her she was nervous about sleeping alone in a strange house. 'I'm going to have to move in with her,' Lydia told Luke, 'and that's not going to work too well for either of us because I need to be up really early in the mornings to get on with the breakfasts.'

He rubbed his chin thoughtfully. 'I know — why not ask Mrs Metcalf if Jodie can share with Maisie just for the time being? After all, it must be quite crowded with five of them in that family room.'

Mrs Metcalf was more than happy with the arrangement and the girls were ecstatic.

Luke showed them how to use the internal phone in case of emergencies, and Mrs Metcalf sensibly removed the kettle and set a few ground rules about the use of the television.

Lydia provided the girls with squash, bottled water and a few biscuits.

'Thanks, Luke,' she told him.

'Whatever for?'

'For being so thoughtful. It's much better arrangement all round but I'm still cross with Nell for swanning off with her friends.'

'Oh, don't be too hard on the girl. After all, this is supposed to be her holiday, too.'

'It's also supposed to be mine!' she reminded him. 'And yours come to that, but we're being responsible. I love Maisie dearly, but like any other child of her age, she needs to be kept occupied.'

'Then I'll need to put on my thinking cap and see what I can come up with in the way of entertainment. You're pretty free after the morning rush is over, aren't you?'

'Yes, and it's been great to have you around to help out but I don't want to impose on either you or the Metcalfs.'

His expression changed. 'I thought we'd got beyond that 'ever so polite, just met you' stage. I had hoped that we were friends but obviously I'm mistaken.'

His gaze met hers unwaveringly and her heart beat wildly.

The moment was broken when

Maisie and Jodie came bursting into the kitchen.

'Jodie's mum says if we go up to our room now we can watch a DVD on her portable player. But we've got to get ready for bed first. So can we, Aunty Lyddie?'

Lydia gave the two small girls a stern look. 'I'm sure that'll be OK, but you mustn't, either of you, ever again come running into the kitchen like that.'

'Why not?' Jodie asked, looking bewildered.

'There are too many things that could get knocked over and burn you while I'm cooking,' Lydia told them.

'But you're not cooking,' Maisie pointed out.

'And there are knives and other sharp things lying around in here,' Luke put in helpfully.

The two girls looked about them, not seeing anything sharp anywhere.

'And you might just get one of these stuck on your head and then we'd have to take you to hospital to get it off.'

Luke grabbed a saucepan from the shelf, put it on his head and then pretended he couldn't remove it.

The two girls doubled up with mirth and Lydia could no longer keep a straight face.

Just then, Mrs Metcalf put her head round the door.

'Jodie, you know you mustn't come into the kitchen.'

She caught sight of Luke and joined in the laughter.

Lydia yanked the saucepan off his head and he yelped and hopped about the kitchen.

'Luke was just demonstrating a point about the dangers in the kitchen but, personally, I think he's missing his vocation.'

Luke rubbed his ear. 'I must take after my Uncle Joel. He used to be a comedian — like your Uncle Ted. Weird coincidence, eh?'

Lydia stared at him. 'I thought Joel had been in business.'

'So he was — show business. In fact,

while he's away on the cruise, he's been offered two or three slots in the entertainment programme. Oh, yes, Joel Norris was very popular on the comedy circuit at one time. He used to travel all over the place but he had to ease off a few years ago when his heart started playing up.'

* * *

The following morning, Luke did his stint with the pancakes and then disappeared back to Willow Cottage.

Lydia made sure Maisie had everything she needed for her outing with the Metcalfs to Trotters World Of Animals, then went upstairs to help Gemma because it was Mrs Dalton's day off.

It was lunch time before Luke reappeared.

Lydia was wearing shorts and a baggy top and her hair was swathed in a scarf.

He smiled at her. 'Sorry to interrupt

you in your chores, Mrs Mop, but I was wondering if you'd care to take a look at the cottage now it's practically finished? That's if you can spare the time, of course.'

'I shan't be free for at least another hour,' Lydia told him.

'Oh, I can finish off here, no worries,' Gemma assured her, leaving her with no choice but to go upstairs and tidy herself up.

When she came back down wearing a denim skirt and a fresh white T-shirt, her hair neatly secured in a scrunchie, Luke was sitting in the sun lounge reading a newspaper.

He looked up and studied her, but made no comment, merely got to his feet and said, 'Right then, shall we go?'

Joel's cottage was halfway up the lane and overlooked the fells.

Although Lydia had been inside it before, she had not been invited beyond the living-room.

Now, she could see, it had been tastefully redecorated. The walls were washed in pastel shades and there were new carpets and curtains. The kitchen was beautifully appointed, full of up-to-date fitments and appliances.

'Come and have a look upstairs,' Luke invited, 'and then I'll get us some lunch.'

Willow Cottage was more spacious than she had realised. The upstairs had newly-fitted wardrobes and bathrooms. And the view from the master bedroom across the fields to the fells was superb.

'It's really lovely — so light and airy. When's Joel hoping to let it out to paying guests?'

'Possibly by the summer. He can always advertise on the internet.'

Returning to the kitchen, he whipped up a couple of fluffy omelettes which he filled with ham and served with a side salad and crisp French bread.

Over lunch, Lydia said, 'I was wondering about taking Maisie and Jodie out tomorrow. Saturday would be better, but Ian Metcalf's mother has invited all the family to tea then.'

'Wouldn't Nell want to go too?'

'I shouldn't think so — she hasn't rung, apart from a quick call to check that Maisie's OK. She's obviously enjoying herself too much with her chums.'

'Well, she knows Maisie's in good hands. Look, why don't I come with you? What had you got in mind?'

'I wondered about taking them to The World Of Beatrix Potter in Bowness. I know Maisie went a couple of years ago but I'm sure she wouldn't mind going again.'

He looked at her thoughtfully. 'You like children, don't you?'

She helped herself to coleslaw. 'Yes, when I can hand them back at the end of the day,' she quipped.

Over coffee, Luke suddenly said, 'So, do you think your aunt will get the urge to fully renovate Hill House once she sees what's been done to Willow Cottage?'

Lydia considered. 'I think she's more concerned with making her guests feel at home than in giving them sumptuous surroundings. She'd rather they could relax than be afraid to flatten the cushions.'

Luke nodded understandingly. 'I think I see what you're getting at, but I know she's aware that Hill House needs refurbishment. I appreciate we need to tread carefully in order not to hurt her feelings, but you've seen the vast improvement the attic conversion has made.'

'Yes, of course, but that's a bit different. You've got to weigh up what Aunt Mattie offers in return for the rates she's charging and I think it's all more than adequate. Turn it into a more upmarket venture and she won't be happy. It just isn't Aunt Mattie.'

'Well, we'll just have to wait and see, won't we?'

She wondered what he meant by that remark but supposed all would be revealed when her aunt returned from her holiday. Until then she would just have to be patient.

Next day, Maisie and Jodie were enthralled by The World Of Beatrix Potter. They revelled in the stories of Peter Rabbit, Mrs Tiggywinkle, Jemima Puddleduck and all the other animals, and talked about the books they had read when they were smaller. Leaving the attraction, they found a teashop in Bowness which served a delicious array of cakes and ice cream, and Luke treated them all.

'When my Aunt Mattie was a girl, she used to visit an old gentleman who had worked on Beatrix Potter's farm,' Lydia told the girls.

'Did he know Beatrix Potter?'

'He did meet her once or twice when she was out walking across the fields.'

'My mum told me she once saw a film about the Tales Of Beatrix Potter when she was up here in the Lake District,' Maisie said, spooning up her ice-cream.

'And now there's a new film about the life of Miss Potter,' Luke informed them.

Somehow this helped to bring it all alive for the girls, who then turned their conversation towards ballet — they both attended dancing classes.

When they arrived back at Hill House, Maisie and Jodie rushed into the house to tell the Metcalf family all about their day out.

'Thanks, Luke,' Lydia said. 'It's been a great day.'

He smiled. 'It's been fun, hasn't it? If anything, I should thank you for letting me tag along. I've enjoyed myself immensely!'

She began to walk towards the house. 'I just wish I lived a bit nearer to Maisie so I could see her more often,' she told him.

'Yes, it's hard when a family is separated,' he remarked and she thought she detected a wistful note in his voice and touched his arm, almost without thinking.

'Do you keep in touch with your mother, Luke?'

His expression changed and a shadow crossed his face.

'No — she made it clear, back when I was a baby, that she didn't want anything to do with me. Look, if you don't mind I'd rather not talk about it. It's a sore subject and I don't want to spoil what has been a lovely day.'

'No, of course not,' she said awkwardly, wishing she'd kept quiet, and was relieved to find Jodie's mum waiting for them in the hall.

'They've had a wonderful time. Thank you so much, you two . . . Lydia, there's been a phone call for you. Mrs Dalton asked me if I'd tell you to be sure to ring back. She's left you a note.'

Mrs Dalton's message on the pad was brief and to the point.

'Someone called Mr Trent rang. Please ring back pronto.'

Lydia immediately felt a bit guilty because she hadn't phoned Trent since she'd been up in Silverdale, knowing he was probably indulging in a fit of the sulks anyway. She decided to ring him later on and turned away from the desk to find that Luke had vanished and realised he was good at that.

* * *

Trent rang again while she was getting Maisie's tea ready.

'It's a terrible line,' she told him. 'You're breaking up!'

She just about caught the words *exhibition, Manchester* and *bank holiday*, before she lost his mobile signal altogether. She tried ringing him back but to no avail. It was about half an hour later before called again and, this time, he used a landline.

'What sort of backwater are you in?' he asked irritably. 'I was trying to tell you I've decided to go to that photographic exhibition in Manchester tomorrow.

'Actually, I'm on my way there now — phoning from a service station. I'm staying over with friends tonight and we're all going together. I thought I could spend the rest of the bank holiday with you — Manchester's not that far away from your aunt's place, is it?

'So why don't you join me in Manchester, Lyddie? There are things we need to sort out and then I'll return with you to the Lakes. I think it's high time I saw this place you've been raving on about for so long.'

This was so unexpected that it totally threw her. She suddenly realised that she didn't want Trent here, in her special place, and she particularly didn't want him around Luke, but she couldn't explain why — even to herself.

For a moment or two, she didn't reply. Then she came to with a start as Trent demanded to know if she was still there.

'Yes, I'm here . . . Trent, listen, I'm sorry, but there's no way I can get to Manchester tomorrow.'

She explained about Maisie.

'Right — well, that's a disappointment but I suppose I half expected it . . . So, can you put me up at your aunt's guesthouse?'

'It's very short notice and we're fully booked. Look, Trent, I'm not sure if it's a good idea for you to come up just now. I really am pretty busy!'

'Stop making excuses! I'll see you tomorrow afternoon,' he said firmly, and put down the phone.

Suddenly, she realised why she didn't want Trent to come to Silverdale. It was because her time there was spent in a kind of bubble, suspended from reality, and Trent's presence would burst that bubble, taking her back to a world that was full of problems.

She also knew that she was enjoying Luke's company more than she was prepared to admit to anyone.

After Maisie had had her tea and was happily playing a board game with Jodie, Lydia called the nearest hotel to see if they could put up Trent for a night or two. Fortunately, they'd had an

117

unexpected cancellation.

She didn't know how she was going to juggle running the guesthouse with looking after Maisie — let alone find time to entertain Trent. But, fortunately, Nell would be taking her small niece out shopping on the following day, so that would give Lydia chance to catch up with a few jobs.

Problems, Problems

Lydia had a restless night, aware she was being pushed into making a decision about her future with Trent before she was ready. She woke up feeling unrefreshed, but much calmer about the situation. She had made up her mind and would not let Trent change it, however persuasive he might be. She realised she was no longer sure of her feelings for him and that there was no way she wanted him to move in with her.

Saturday morning passed in a flash. Several guests left and were replaced by new ones.

Ginny popped in for coffee and, when Lydia told her about Trent's forthcoming visit, she raised her eyebrows.

'You certainly get yourself into some tangles, don't you? Why didn't you just tell him you couldn't see him? After all,

I thought you needed a bit more time to sort yourself out.'

'I don't need any more time, I've made my decision,' Lydia told her friend, 'and, before you ask, the answer's, no!'

Ginny gave her a searching look. 'So you say now, but when he's actually here in front of you, perhaps you'll think again.'

Would she? Lydia wished things weren't so complicated. She realised she ought to have dissuaded Trent from coming, but knew she had to face him some time.

'Well, the next few days should prove interesting,' Ginny commented. 'What time's he arriving?'

'That depends on how good the exhibition proves to be.'

★ ★ ★

In fact, Trent arrived shortly after Maisie and Nell returned from their day out.

120

Lydia had sent Maisie off to change before joining the Metcalfs on the playing field, and she and Nell were chatting in the entrance hall when Trent pulled up in his red Mazda sports car. Excusing herself, she went out to greet him.

'Well, this is the back of beyond, isn't it?' he said, after giving her a swift kiss. 'How on earth do people survive up here? It's like stepping back in time. When I stopped at a hotel to ask the way just now, they were shooing sheep out of the car park. You can't seriously tell me you like it here, after being in Canterbury!'

'That's just where you're wrong — I absolutely love it!' she informed him, stung by his criticism. 'I like Canterbury, too, of course, but, actually, there's no comparison.'

Nell came down the steps just then. 'Aren't you going to introduce me, Lydia? Although I suspect this must be Trent.'

Trent gave her an engaging smile

and, taking her hand, held it fractionally longer than was necessary. 'Let me guess — you're Nell. Lydia didn't tell me what a looker you are! You have the most beautiful bone structure!'

Luke appeared at that moment from the direction of Willow Cottage, and the two men looked enquiringly at each other.

'Luke, this is my friend and business partner, Trent Symons, and this, Trent, is Luke Carstairs, the nephew of a friend of my aunt. Luke's helping me run the guesthouse while she's away.'

The two men acknowledged each other and Trent said, 'Right then. Maybe you could show me to my room, Lydia?'

'I'm sorry, but I've booked you into the hotel down the road. I told you we didn't have a spare room here. And, to be honest, we're so busy that I won't be able to see much of you.'

'This wasn't how I'd planned it,' he said crossly. 'I left the exhibition earlier than I'd intended so's I'd have more time to spend with you.' He turned to Luke, who was listening to the conversation with interest. 'Perhaps you could step in, Luke, while I take Lydia out to dinner? We've got a few things to discuss in private.'

'Why not,' Luke said pleasantly. 'I'm not planning on doing anything this evening.'

'But you're expected to have your dinner at the hotel, Trent,' Lydia told him, feeling embarrassed that he had dragged Luke into their affairs.

'So? They can give us a table for two and we can both eat there,' he pointed out.

★ ★ ★

Trent was at his most charming during the meal, telling her about the photographic exhibition and passing on the good wishes of his friends, whom Lydia had met once or twice and found rather loud. But, as soon as they were seated in a corner of the bar, he turned the conversation to their future together.

'I was hoping your time here would make you realise just how much you were missing me,' he began. 'So have you come to a decision?' His pale-blue eyes looked at her intently.

She swallowed, knowing he wasn't going to like what she had to say.

'I'm sorry, Trent. But my flat is small and I like my own space.'

He downed his drink as if his life depended on it. 'I thought you cared about me.'

'Of course I do, and it's difficult for me to say this but . . .'

'Go on,' he prompted, his eyes glinting dangerously.

'Well, to be honest, I don't think living with you is what I want. I thought you knew me well enough to realise that — for me — commitment means everything.'

He frowned. 'You're not making sense, Lyddie. I'm asking you to make a commitment by letting me move in with you!'

'No,' she said firmly. 'You're not. The reason you want to move in with me is because you're fed up with sharing a flat with a couple of uncouth youths! You've told me often enough. It would just be a convenience for you!'

He looked fit to explode and she was heartily relieved when Bridget, the hotel owner, came over to ask if they had enjoyed their meal and to find out if Lydia could find a spare evening to take some photographs of the guests.

Trent could be perfectly charming when he chose, and he gave Bridget the full benefit of his smile, complimenting her on the meal and offering to do the photographs himself the following evening.

When she had gone he turned back to Lydia.

'It's getting crowded in here — let's go up to my room and talk some more.'

She shook her head. 'No, Trent. It's getting late and it's high time I was going.'

'Running away?' he demanded nastily.

'No, of course not, but the guesthouse is my responsibility — I did warn you I'd be busy. Besides, there's Maisie to think about.'

'I thought Luke was taking care of everything? Who is that guy anyway?'

'I've told you. He's Joel's nephew.'

'Well, he seems to like throwing his weight about,' Trent commented unfairly. 'Does he live in Silverdale?'

'No, he lives in London. He's been staying at Hill House while the builders have been doing renovations to his uncle's cottage — it's his uncle who's away on holiday with my aunt.'

She didn't want to discuss Luke with Trent or divulge too much of her family affairs.

'Thanks for dinner. I'll see you tomorrow. Goodnight.'

'Don't go. I'll be lonely,' he told her plaintively.

'Don't be ridiculous!' she told him crisply, and then added, more softly,

'Look, we've both had a long day and I've got to be up early tomorrow. I'll see you after breakfast — say around ten-thirty?

And he had to be content with that.

★ ★ ★

Luke was talking to Mr Jones in the visitors' lounge when Lydia arrived back at Hill House.

The old man was just getting to his feet. 'Well, I think I'll retire to bed,' he said. 'I need to get my beauty sleep. See you both tomorrow.'

'Did you have a good evening?' Luke asked her as the door closed behind the departing guest.

'Yes, thank you. Bridget is a superb cook. Did Nell stay to help you here?'

'Yes, she's only just gone, as a matter of fact, and she said she'll come back tomorrow. We thought perhaps the pair of us could take Maisie out and give you and Trent some quality time together.'

That was the last thing Lydia wanted. 'Well, it's very thoughtful of you both, but I wouldn't want Maisie to feel she's an inconvenience to me. After all, Trent only decided to come up here at the last minute, and I am responsible for my niece, as he well knows.'

'Well, it's up to you, of course, but the offer's there.' He gave her a shrewd look. 'It doesn't seem to me as if you've enjoyed your evening as much as you're making out.'

Lydia returned his look, thinking that he could not be nearer to the truth.

'I've had a very pleasant time — not that it's any business of yours.'

'None at all,' he agreed. 'I'll see you in the morning.'

The following morning the heavens opened and Trent appeared at about ten o'clock, looking sullen.

'I can't imagine what you see in this place. It's so grey and gloomy.'

'But when the sun shines it's unbelievably beautiful — a complete transformation,' she told him.

'I'll take your word for it — so what are we doing today?'

'I'm afraid I'll be busy for another hour or so, and then there's Maisie to consider.'

Nell turned up about half an hour later, looking enchanting in kingfisher blue. Trent gazed at her appreciatively.

'I so enjoyed taking Maisie out yesterday that I thought I'd spend today with her as well. I'm sure you'd welcome a bit of time with Trent, Lyddie, especially as he's only here for such a short time.'

Maisie was playing in the lounge with the Metcalf children, under the watchful eye of their father.

Lydia made some coffee and went back to her chores.

When she returned, shortly afterwards, it was to find Nell and Trent deep in conversation.

'Trent says he'd like to use me as a model for some of his photographs.'

'She's got amazing bone structure. I've said I'll do a modelling portfolio for her in exchange.'

Lydia suddenly realised why Nell had been so keen to come over to Hill House that morning. She was obviously aware of the work Trent produced and had her eye to the main chance. Jenny had once told Lydia that her sister-in-law had aspirations to become a model, but that her mother had insisted she should get her media studies degree first.

Maisie came running in at that point. 'The Metcalfs are going to see their grandma now, so what's happening to me?' She stopped in her tracks as she caught sight of Trent.

'Oh, hello! Aunty said you came yesterday, but I didn't see you.'

Trent mumbled something about being invisible and Maisie giggled.

'So who's taking me out today?' she demanded, as Luke entered the room.

He greeted everyone with his usual charm, before turning to the small girl in front of him. 'Well, Maisie, Nell and I thought perhaps you'd like to come out with us this morning.'

'Great — but why can't we all go out together?'

'Well, you see, angel, Aunty Lyddie and Trent want to talk to each other,' Nell explained.

Maisie looked from one to the other and then light suddenly dawned.

'Oh, secrets. Grown-ups always have secrets! OK, is it shops again?'

Nell got to her feet. 'We'll see — go and get your anorak.'

She gave Trent a devastating smile. 'I've had an idea. Why don't we go our separate ways for the rest of the morning, then all meet up somewhere for lunch?'

★ ★ ★

Lydia and Trent set off in his sports car on a tour of the southern Lakes. The rain slowed to a fine drizzle, and they managed to cover a lot of ground.

'Aren't there any cinemas or theatres

round here?' he asked peevishly, obviously unimpressed by the landscape. 'We could at least go to see a decent film.'

Lydia put her foot down at that, but she could see he wasn't the least bit interested in the scenery. It seemed that even when it cleared up and a watery sun came out, nothing could improve his mood and, after a time, she gave up trying. They just didn't seem to be on the same wavelength any more.

To her surprise, however, when they met up with the others at Skelwith Bridge for a late lunch, he went out of his way to be the life and soul of the party. Nell had obviously captivated him and it seemed to Lydia that he could hardly keep his eyes off her. Nell was getting on rather well with Luke, too.

Later in the afternoon, after the five of them had walked round Grasmere together, Lydia, Maisie and Luke went to browse around one of the galleries. Maisie was very artistic for a young child and, after admiring the paintings, they purchased some postcards.

'Nell's gone ahead with Trent. Apparently, they're keen to look at a couple of shops over there before they close.' Luke pointed in the general direction the pair had been heading.

'Right,' Lydia scooped up her purchases and they made their way out of the gallery and back to the car park.

'This isn't turning out to be the best of days for you, is it?' he asked, as Maisie ran on ahead of them.

'I don't know what you mean,' she told him, her heart thumping as he linked her arm in his.

He sighed. 'I've tried to keep Nell out of your hair as much as possible, but she's determined to get that portfolio Trent's mentioned, and I suspect she's arranging a sitting with him, right now.'

'That's OK. Trent always has an eye for opportunities and he's right — Nell is very photogenic.'

Luke smiled. 'That's very generous of you — so you don't mind being saddled with me for a bit?'

'Why should I?' she asked lightly. 'I see plenty of Trent when I'm in Canterbury and you and Nell have been more than good with Maisie.'

'She's a great little kid . . . When's your sister arriving?'

'I'm not too sure — soon, I hope, or she won't get any time up here at all.'

Maisie came running back to them at that point.

When they got to the car park, Trent's car had gone. Luke frowned, but Lydia said brightly, 'Not to worry, I expect they got tired of waiting.'

* * *

Nell and Trent didn't appear for a full half-hour after the others arrived back. Nell was laughing at something Trent had said and was clutching a garish carrier bag. They seemed surprised at Lydia's obvious annoyance.

'I knew you weren't listening,' Nell chided, fluttering her lashes. 'I said we'd stop off at Rheged on the way back because I saw something I liked in one of the shops there yesterday. Anyway, we've had a great time, in spite of the weather. Did I tell you Trudi and Rob are asking a few folk round tonight and you're all invited?'

The two men had wandered out of earshot.

'No, you were obviously speaking to someone else. Look, Nell, I'd like to come but . . .'

Nell looked annoyed. 'There's always a but, isn't there? Why don't you get yourself a life, Lydia?'

Stunned by this attack, Lydia retorted, 'In case it's escaped your notice, there are Aunt Mattie's guests to consider! You kindly kept an eye on Maisie last night, but tonight I need to be around at Hill House — so thanks, but no thanks — with apologies to your friends. There is, however, nothing to stop Trent from joining you.'

There was a pause, and then Nell said sweetly, 'Don't be silly, as if I'd take your boyfriend away from you . . . I'll see what Luke's doing.'

Much to Lydia's surprise, Luke accepted the invitation, and when Nell phoned her friends they told her to take him to dinner as well.

Life was full of surprises, Lydia told herself, not all of them good ones.

Just then the Metcalfs' car appeared and, as the children tumbled out, Maisie shot off to speak to her friends.

'And then there were two,' Trent said in her ear.

'Three, actually,' she corrected him, watching her small niece.

'Oh, she'll be tucked up in bed, surely, so you can come over to the hotel for dinner like last night.'

She shook her head. 'Sorry, Trent. That's just not on.'

She saw the sulky expression on his face, and sensed his mood.

'Oh, don't look like that. If you like, I'll ring Bridget at the hotel and see if I can persuade her to let us have some of her lovely food to take away.'

He brightened. 'That's a brilliant idea — then we can have a proper tête-à-tête undisturbed.'

'No, Trent. Maisie will be eating with us. She needs to be fed, too.'

He shook off her arm. 'You're making things very difficult, Lydia. It's almost as if you don't want to be alone with me.'

She gave a little laugh. 'Don't be ridiculous! Look, you can either accept the situation or eat on your own at the hotel!'

He looked at her in astonishment. 'I'm beginning to wish I'd gone with Nell and Luke. I think I'd have had more fun. You need to chill out, Lydia!'

'Sorry to be such boring company. It's not too late for you to join the others — they haven't left yet but, in case it's slipped your mind, you promised Bridget you'd take photographs of her hotel guests tonight.'

She'd called his bluff and, after a moment or two, he said sullenly, 'Yes. Right. OK. I'm going to the hotel to change — I'll be back in about an hour.'

Lydia phoned the hotel and, in due course, Bridget sent her eldest son along with several containers of food and Lydia, Trent and Maisie sat down to an excellent meal.

Maisie was full of her day out and chattered away over her chicken cacciatore. Trent, however, was uncharacteristically quiet, while Lydia's mind was filled with a mixture of thoughts.

She'd been taken aback to realise that Trent wasn't keen on children. The subject had never arisen before — it was still early days in their relationship — but he'd always seemed fine, both with the children who were having their photographs taken in the studio and those in the schools they visited.

She supposed that when it was work it was different from now, when he was expected to entertain Maisie, and this did not bode well for the future of their relationship because Lydia knew that she would want children, and that deep down, she was longing to have a family of her own.

As they sampled Bridget's delectable desserts, Maisie suddenly clapped her hand to her mouth. 'Oops! I forgot to tell you, Aunty Lyddie! Mummy rang while you were upstairs. She's coming tomorrow for definite. Grandma's much better now.'

'Well, that is good news, darling. I'll call her back once we've finished eating,' Lydia said, relieved to know that her sister would be with her shortly.

Trent set down his spoon. 'If Jenny's coming up here, then there's no need for you to stay on any longer, is there?'

Lydia stared at him. 'You really don't get it, do you Trent? I love it here and I'm planning to stay until Aunt Mattie and Joel return from their cruise.

They fell into silence and, after a minute or two, Maisie — who'd finished her banoffee pie — asked, 'Can I go and find Jodie, now?'

'Just for half an hour or so and then it's bedtime.'

'So what are we going to do?' Trent asked after Maisie had gone.

'I'm going to wash up so that you can take back the dishes to the hotel, and then you've got an assignation with a camera.'

'I don't recognise this new domesticated you,' he complained. 'I thought perhaps we could relax over a bottle of wine.'

She shook her head. 'I did a deal with Bridget. She agreed to provide the dinner if you provide the photographs — don't worry, you can still charge the guests for them — so you'd better get cracking. You can have your drink over there.'

He pulled a face. 'And you'll join me when you've put the infant to bed?'

She sighed. 'Maisie is quite capable of putting herself to bed, but there's no way I can go out and leave her. I'm afraid you have two options Trent — either stay at Bridget's or come back here for the rest of the evening.'

He made a move towards her, a

gleam in his eyes, and enfolded her tightly in his arms.

'You know, I think I'm beginning to like this new, assertive Lydia,' he said, and kissed her hard. Then there was a loud rap on the door and she hastily straightened her blouse. Trent said something rude under his breath.

One of the new guests stood outside the door. 'So sorry to disturb you, Miss Lawson, but I was wondering if you had any navy thread? My button's dropped off.'

Lydia tried not to giggle. Then she found the thread and finished the washing-up, while Trent made coffee and complained bitterly that she was neglecting him.

She was stung by this. 'That's unfair! You know full well I came up here for a working holiday. Life isn't one long round of nightclubs!'

'You know what, Lydia? You're no fun any more. Perhaps I've found out just in time! You ought to take a leaf out of Nell's book. She's obviously a girl who likes a good time!'

Lydia did not reply for a few moments. She felt inexplicably hurt by this attack.

At last she told him, 'Nell's rather younger than me, and just because I face up to my responsibilities, it doesn't mean to say that I don't enjoy a good time too. Actually, I think you're being a bit self-centred, but then you always did like your own way!'

'What!' His face turned red. 'Well, I think you're in danger of becoming an old spinster like . . . like . . . '

'Go on,' she invited, biting back her anger.

'Like your Aunt Janet!'

She gasped. 'Trent that is so unfair! For a start you have never met my Aunt Janet, but if you had, you'd know she's a lovely lady and, quite apart from that, she's no blood relation of mine, anyway.'

He picked up the dishes that he was to return to the hotel. 'I'll see you in the morning when you've had a chance to cool down and think about what I've said.'

When he'd gone, she finished tidying up, venting her feelings by banging the cupboard doors, and when she'd calmed down a little, she rang Jenny.

Her sister was apologetic when Lydia relayed what had happened.

'Oh, Lyddie it's all my fault! If I'd been there, you could have gone out with Trent and this situation wouldn't have arisen.'

'It's probably just as well it has. There's a side to him that I've never seen before and there are obviously things about me that he'd not noticed either. I don't think we're nearly as compatible as I'd thought, and I'm not even sure he likes children.'

There was a pause and then Jenny said, 'Lyddie that's crazy, he works with them on a regular basis!'

'I know, but the school photographs

bring in a good income so he'd be bound to make a supreme effort. Anyway, I'm looking forward to seeing you tomorrow.'

'Don't do anything rash, love. Think things through properly,' Jenny cautioned.

Lydia was now faced with the problem of where to put her sister. She didn't want to turn Jodie out of Maisie's room for the one remaining night that the Metcalfs were staying at Hill House, but her problem was resolved by Luke, who came in around elevenish and told her he'd be moving back to Willow Cottage the following day, since the work there was just about complete.

★　★　★

The next morning was glorious and Lydia suggested that perhaps Trent might join her and Maisie on a walk. He quickly rejected this idea by saying that he didn't have the right shoes for the terrain.

'Right — well, I tell you what then, let's take Maisie to the Ullswater steamer. She's always happy to do that.'

But Maisie refused to go without Jodie Metcalf and, seeing the resigned look on Trent's face, Lydia realised this was going to be a difficult excursion.

To give him his due, he did make an effort to be nice to the girls, but it was obvious that he wasn't keen on children.

He couldn't understand why they couldn't be allowed to go up on deck on their own, while he and Lydia drank coffee in the lounge.

The sun shone that morning showing the lake in all its glory. The mountain scenery was spectacular. She pointed out Helvellyn and one or two other landmarks, but they all failed to impress Trent.

When they arrived back at Hill House, Nell was there, chatting away to Luke over coffee.

'I thought you and Trent might welcome a couple of hours to yourselves, as he's leaving this afternoon,' she said sweetly, and Lydia had no alternative but to agree to her looking after Maisie.

Lydia and Trent went to Patterdale where they sat over lunch in a delightful hotel. To her it was idyllic.

'Have you changed your mind about the Lakes?' she asked him presently.

'If you mean, do I like the place any better, now that I've seen it in fine weather, then no, I don't. And I can't imagine why you'd want to bury yourself away in this boring dump at your age.

'Personally, I'd be bored out of my skull within a week. Quite apart from not being able to stand all the rain, I don't like mountains — I find them oppressive and can't understand why people want to climb them. It's like stepping back into a bygone era up here. It's bad enough at this time of the year. Whatever is it like in the winter?'

Lydia was stunned and hurt. This was her special place and he was maligning it.

'Surely,' she said, in a small voice, 'there must be something about the Lakes that you've enjoyed while you've been here?'

He considered. 'Well, the food's pretty good, I'll grant you that — and that girl, Nell, has got something going for her. She's very photogenic — lots of potential.'

He drained his wine glass. 'Have you thought over what we've been discussing, Lyddie?'

She finished her dessert, resolving to remain calm. 'I don't believe there's anything further to discuss,' she said decisively. 'The answer's still no.'

He didn't look surprised, or even as if he cared too much, but watching her intently said, 'Perhaps you could, at least, give me a bit more of an explanation than you have so far?'

She sighed. 'I thought I knew you, Trent, but now I don't think I do, after all. We seem to be poles apart on some issues and I'm afraid it just wouldn't work.'

He gave a short laugh. 'The whole idea of living together would be so's we could find out more about each other — but if that's your decision, then it's going to make it a tad awkward for us to continue working together.'

'It needn't,' she told him, and sat toying with the stem of her glass as his words sank in.

He gave her a long, hard look from ice-blue eyes. 'Well, you surely don't expect us to carry on as if nothing's happened between us?'

'So what exactly do you propose we do?' she asked dully, as the full impact of what he was saying hit her.

He shrugged. 'For the time being, I suppose I've no alternative but to continue working at the studio, but as soon as I can, I'll be looking for new premises and for a new business partner!'

An Evening With Luke

After Trent had dropped her off with a murmured goodbye, Lydia stormed into Hill House, her face set. Luke appeared from nowhere as usual.

'Lover's tiff?' he asked mildly.

'None of your business,' she snapped.

He raised his eyebrows. 'Pardon me! Though I must say, he seemed a nice enough guy, but totally like a fish out of water here.'

Not trusting herself to speak, she stomped into the office, pointedly shutting the door. She wanted to confide in him, but pride wouldn't let her.

An hour later, Jenny arrived.

Lydia gave her a hug. 'Am I glad to see you!'

'My mother-in-law insisted I should drive up this morning, before I encountered all the traffic — where's Maisie?'

'In the garden playing with the

Metcalfs — Luke and one or two of the other guests seem to be joining in. You've just missed Nell.'

Luke had unearthed the dressing-up box from the cupboard in his bedroom and there was a crazy game of pirates going on in the garden. Jenny chuckled as she watched from the window and, after a few moments, she and Lydia went outside.

Maisie came racing over to give Jenny a hug, saying, 'Mummy, I'm having such a brill time! Luke, come and say hello to my mum.'

Luke obligingly came across. He was wearing an eyepatch and a hat adorned with a skull and crossbones, and was wielding a rather bendy plastic sword, but seemed oblivious to his appearance as he stuck out his free hand to shake Jenny's.

'Hello, Maisie's mum. I'm Luke Carstairs — Joel's nephew.'

Jenny shook his hand. 'Hello, Luke. I like the hat, and the eyepatch is very fetching!'

Maisie giggled and Luke, suddenly aware of what he must look like, gave a bellow of laughter and swept off his hat with a flourish.

The Metcalfs came across for a chat with Jenny, and Lydia disappeared into the house to make tea and to find lemonade for the children.

★ ★ ★

'Maisie will be devastated when the Metcalfs go home tomorrow. She gets on so well with them, especially Jodie,' Lydia remarked as she sat on her sister's bed while Jenny unpacked a few things for her overnight stay in the room that Luke had vacated. Once Jodie Metcalf had gone home, she'd move in with Maisie.

'I know, but she'll see them all again in the summer.' Jenny gave her a concerned look. 'You're looking peaky, Lyddie. What's up?'

Lydia told her briefly what had happened with Trent.

'Well, if you don't want him to move in with you, then you're right not to go along with it. After all, it could prove to be the biggest mistake of your life!'

The tears welled up in Lydia's eyes. 'The problem is, Trent says he doesn't see how we can carry on working together, and you know how long it took me to find someone to share the studio after Anthea left.'

'Lydia that's emotional blackmail! Trent can't be a very nice person!'

Lydia dabbed at her eyes with a soggy tissue. 'I thought he was — I really did, until now — but he doesn't like the Lakes. I mean — how can anyone not like the Lakes?'

Jenny smiled sympathetically. 'He's a townie, love. Some people can't cope with open spaces, any more than others can cope with built-up areas. But you have a good working relationship, don't you?'

'Yes, in the main, although we don't see eye to eye in some areas.'

'How d'you mean?' Jenny popped

some T-shirts into a drawer and turned to face her sister.

'Well, you know he does portfolios for models?'

Jenny nodded. 'I realise you've never been very happy about that, although you've never said as much.'

Lydia hesitated. 'Sometimes he does commissions for a friend and that involves the girls modelling rather skimpy swimwear — or he might do a photo shoot for a firm that sells lingerie.'

'I see — more on the tacky side than you would approve of, eh?'

'Put like that you make me sound like a prude and I'm not. It's just that I'd rather he didn't involve the name of our studio with that kind of work.'

Jenny gave her a searching glance. 'Has he ever asked you to model for him?'

'Only once, but I told him quite definitely that I'd be sticking to photography and he got the message

. . . but he's offered to do a portfolio for Nell.'

Jenny whistled. 'I bet she jumped at the opportunity.'

As her sister brushed her mane of fair hair in front of the mirror, Lydia picked up a framed photograph that Luke had left on the bedside table and, studying it closely, her eyes widened.

'Have you seen this photo of Luke's family, Jenny?' she asked slowly.

Jenny took a look. 'What a happy crowd! There's Joel and I suppose the other people must be the rest of his family.'

'Yes, I assume so — but take a good look at that woman. I'm sure there's something familiar about her.' She frowned with concentration. 'I'm sure I've seen her somewhere before, but I can't place her.'

Jenny took a closer look. 'Yes, you're right. She does remind me of someone.'

Lydia snapped her fingers. 'You know, I've got a strange feeling I've seen another photo of this woman, and

I'm sure I've seen it somewhere in this house! There used to be several photograph albums lying about up here when it was an attic. I remember Uncle Ted showing them to me.'

'Well, you're the expert when it comes to photos. But if you're so interested, why not just ask Luke who she is? Maybe it's his mother?'

Lydia shrugged. 'I doubt it. It seems she didn't want anything to do with him, right from when he was a tiny baby — he got quite uptight when I mentioned her. Actually, I think he's a bit of an enigma. He's asked a lot of questions about our family, but isn't keen to divulge too much about himself. He's obviously very fond of Joel, and equally as wary of his uncle's friendship with Aunt Mattie as we are about hers with his uncle.'

Jenny pursed her lips. 'Well, if Mum and Dad aren't bothered then perhaps we ought to leave well alone.'

Lydia was frankly surprised by her sister's attitude. 'But you hear these stories, don't you, about men who prey on wealthy widows?'

'Lyddie, I really don't think Aunt Mattie is a wealthy widow. I would think any capital she might have is tied up in Hill House. I think you're making too much of it, love. You always did have a vivid imagination! Now, I'm going to see Ginny. I want to get a gift for the Metcalfs to thank them for taking Maisie out and about. Are you coming?'

'No, I'll stay here and prepare our supper,' Lydia told her.

★　★　★

She had a lot to think about. It seemed as if she was the only one in the family to be concerned about Aunt Mattie. And it seemed that Luke was equally as troubled by the situation as she was. She encountered him in the kitchen doing a pile of washing-up.

'There's a casserole in the oven for your evening meal tonight,' he told her.

She sniffed appreciatively. 'Luke, you shouldn't have gone to all that trouble — aren't you eating with us?'

'No, I'll take a helping back to the cottage. There are a few things I need to sort out before Uncle Joel gets back at the end of the week.'

Standing watching him as he finished the dishes, Lydia couldn't help comparing him with Trent. They were completely different. Luke was so much more mature. Beside him, Trent paled into insignificance. She knew that what Jenny had said was true — that she and Trent would never have made a go of it — and she bit her lip, wondering why she always made such bad choices where men were concerned.

Jenny came into the kitchen just as Luke was leaving.

'Was it something I said?' she asked.

'No. He says he's got a few things to do before Joel gets back, but he's probably just being tactful and giving us a chance to catch up.'

'Seems like a nice guy,' Jenny said,

giving her sister a meaningful look and Lydia busied herself at the cooker, afraid of giving herself away.

'Oh, he can be completely charming, but I get the distinct impression that there's more to Luke Carstairs than meets the eye.'

'Whereas Trent is rather shallow. I know which one of them I prefer.'

'Even if I did like Luke in that way, I suspect he's already got a girlfriend back in London. Anyway, at least Trent's always straight with me so at least I know where I stand with him,' Lydia said lightly, hoping her sister would drop the subject.

Jenny opened her eyes wide. 'Lyddie if you believe that, then you're even more naïve than I thought. I wasn't going to tell you this, but when I went to the shop, Nell's car was parked outside Bridget's, and if Trent's is a snazzy red sports car then his was alongside it.'

Lydia swallowed. Trent had said he was leaving as soon as he'd paid his hotel bill.

'So? I expect she was just arranging her appointment at the studio — making sure that he meant what he said. After all, Nell always seems to have her eye to the main chance.'

Jenny nodded. 'I guess so — but don't let him manipulate you, Lyddie. This situation is hardly likely to go away now, is it?'

★ ★ ★

After dinner, the two sisters sat talking over cups of coffee until, looking at her watch, Jenny said, 'It's long past Maisie's bedtime. I'd better go and sort her out! So, you're off to a photo session tomorrow evening?'

Lydia nodded. 'Luke might want to come. He's expressed an interest.'

'Well, there you are then — take him up on it while you've got the chance. A man who cooks like a dream and can entertain children, to say nothing of having such a charming personality, is quite a find!'

'You've got it all wrong. He's only interested from the point of view of sussing out the hotel. So far as I'm concerned, I've got about as much appeal for him as a plate of cold custard!'

'I like cold custard,' Maisie announced, bursting into the room, 'so where is it?'

'You'll have to ask Uncle Luke,' Jenny said wickedly. 'Now come on, poppet, it's well past your bedtime and the Metcalfs have got a long day tomorrow!'

★　★　★

Next morning, although he'd said he had a lot to do that day and so wouldn't be around much, Luke came in to make one final batch of pancakes for the Metcalfs and to say goodbye to them. 'What time are you leaving for the hotel tonight?' he asked Lydia, as he was going out of the door.

'Around six forty-five,' she told him, her heart inexplicably pounding.

'Right, I'll see you then — that's if I'm still invited.'

She didn't remind him that he'd actually invited himself, but smiled and said, 'Of course; I'll tell the hotel to expect two of us for dinner.'

Later that morning she went to see Anthea and helped her select some photographs for the forthcoming exhibition.

'I'm afraid I haven't chosen my own yet,' she confessed.

'Too distracted by that nice Luke?' Anthea enquired.

Lydia coloured. 'No, of course not! It's just been so hectic at Hill House and then — I haven't told you — Trent came to visit unexpectedly over the weekend.'

Anthea raised her eyebrows. 'I wouldn't have thought Silverdale was his scene.'

'Too right — it was a bit of a disaster. It looks as if we've split up,' she told her friend.

Anthea set down the photographs.

'You did sort of hint that things weren't working out too well, so I can't say I'm that surprised. From the little I've seen of him, he doesn't seem your type.'

'Yes, well, I'm in big trouble. He's talking of pulling out of the studio and I'll never keep the place going on my own.'

Anthea poured some coffee and came to sit at the table with her friend.

'Now, hang on a minute, Lyddie. He can't just leave you high and dry. He hasn't got a new job, has he?'

'Not so far as I'm aware of, no, but he's got a lot of contacts and perhaps he genuinely feels it's time to move on.'

'And you, what do you feel?' Anthea gave her an intense look.

Lydia sighed. 'I'm not sure. That's the problem. I realise now that although I'm fond of him, I don't love him any more, but I thought we could stay good friends.'

'And I take it he doesn't want that?'

'No — he's taken my decision very badly, although I suspect I've just dented his pride.'

'He'll get over it and when he'd had a chance to think things through, he'll realise what a fool he'd be to let go of that studio.'

'I hope you're right. Things have been going well for me recently with my own projects, but we've still got a lot of contracts for schools — things that we do as a partnership. You and I had begun to build them up and they sort of escalated. If he joined forces with someone else — well I realise competition is healthy but, frankly, I couldn't manage on my own.'

'Well, I'd cross that bridge when I come to it, if I were you,' Anthea said briskly. 'You and I have always worked well as a team. If it got to the point where you'd consider moving, give me a buzz before you look for something else — you could come and work from my studio, even if it's only for a temporary spell. You helped me out once and I'd certainly do the same for you.'

It was something that had never even entered Lydia's head. It was as if a great weight had been lifted off her shoulders. 'Anthea that would be wonderful! If things deteriorated, I could always let out the entire studio to Trent, while casting around for something else.'

'And the flat?'

Lydia shook her head. 'I'm not sure . . . It would need a lot of thinking through.'

'OK. I wouldn't rush you into making any decisions, but the offer's there.'

Lydia left Anthea's studio with a much lighter heart than she'd had for the last few days, and went off to do a bit of retail therapy in Keswick before returning to her aunt's guesthouse.

* * *

That evening, she changed into black trousers and a sparkly top that she'd bought during her shopping trip. She put on her makeup carefully and

164

sprayed on a little perfume.

'You look pretty,' Maisie told her.

Luke came to collect her exactly on time, something that Trent had rarely been able to achieve.

'Well,' he said. 'You scrub up well, Mrs Mop!'

Maisie giggled and Jenny said, 'That's my rôle for a couple of days. I think Lydia's done her fair share of cleaning.'

'Luke's helped,' she pointed out, smiling at him and thinking how handsome he looked in a dark suit and green silk shirt. 'He was a great hit with the children and, as we know, his cooking is wonderful.'

Maisie suddenly remembered something. 'Mummy said to ask you what you did with the cold custard.'

Luke looked mystified, Lydia's cheeks turned pink and Jenny said quickly, 'It was a joke, Luke. Maisie loves cold custard.'

'I won't ask,' Luke said. 'But I'll make you some tomorrow, Maisie — I promise. Come on, Lydia — let's hit the town!'

★ ★ ★

The hotel was situated at Portinscale, a couple of miles west of Keswick and, although the evenings were lengthening, by the time they arrived it was dusk.

There were steps leading up to the entrance and Luke took Lydia's arm as they made their way into the hotel.

Her pulse quickened and — aware of the cool clean fragrance of his cologne and the warmth emanating from his body — she realised that she wasn't as impervious to this man's charms as she made out.

There was an excellent chef at the hotel, and dinner was superb, although Lydia preferred Bridget's more simple but wholesome fare.

She wondered what Luke was thinking as he cast a professional eye over the dining-room and studied the menu.

In between courses, she did her stint with the camera. She always tried to take a casual approach, realising that some people would prefer to have their photographs taken later in the evening during the entertainment, and respected their wishes.

'So what do you think?' she asked Luke when she rejoined him.

'This place has certainly got a nice atmosphere, but I'll give you my final opinion later,' he told her. 'For now, let's just enjoy the food.'

'When you go out for a meal, I suppose you can't help but compare it with the standard of cooking where you work?'

He smiled. 'Yes, it could certainly become a bad habit. But I bet you find yourself studying everything in sight to see if it would make a good photograph.'

She grinned. 'Touché. Actually, I'd like to take your photograph — if you don't mind, of course.'

She studied him unobtrusively as

they ate their dessert. He had a strong profile. His brown eyes were expressive and his smile made her go weak at the knees.

She realised that now was the opportunity to find out more about him, but didn't want to spoil their evening by asking the wrong questions.

He looked up suddenly. 'You know, when you relax, you're totally different,' he told her. 'If I might make an observation, I'm not sure that Trent is right for you.'

She was annoyed by this personal remark, but then she realised that he wouldn't know she and Trent had split up.

'You don't know anything about Trent,' she told him tight-lipped, 'and I know a great deal more about him than I know about you!'

He looked surprised by her response. 'Touched a raw nerve, have I? Let's not spoil an enjoyable evening by bickering.'

'This evening is a working evening

168

for both of us,' she told him sharply.

'Are you a workaholic or what? It seems to me you're in danger of forgetting how to enjoy yourself. You should take a leaf out of Nell's book. She knows how to have a good time.'

Fortunately, at that point, a couple came over to say they had somehow missed out on the photographs and could she oblige. With a little smile directed at Luke, she got to her feet and left the table.

To her amazement, when she returned she found him deep in conversation with Nell who had appeared from nowhere.

'Hi, Lyddie. When I dropped in at Hill House, Jenny told me where you were, so here I am. I'm going back home the day after tomorrow, so I was hoping you'd both come round to Rob and Trudi's tomorrow evening.' Nell fluttered her lashes at Luke.

'Actually, I seem to remember you promised to take Maisie to visit them, and I'm sure Jenny would enjoy a night out,' Lydia told her. She caught Luke's gaze and was aware that he must be thinking she'd just proved him right about her not knowing how to have a good time.

'Oh, Jenny and Maisie are coming over in the morning. It's all arranged.'

Reluctantly, Lydia found herself agreeing to the night out. Shortly afterwards, they all went into the lounge and, over coffee, Nell said, 'So when are you planning to return to London, Luke?'

His face gave nothing away. 'I haven't decided yet. I expect to be here until Uncle Joel and Mrs Lawson return.'

'I'm sure Jenny and Lydia are grateful for all the help and support you've given them.' She simpered at him, treating him to another of her beguiling smiles. Her white dress, simplicity itself and expensively cut, revealed her trim figure. Her blonde hair shone like molten gold.

Lydia got to her feet again, suddenly anxious to get away.

'If you'll excuse me, I'm going to

compliment the chef on the meal, and the staff always like me to do a few photographs just for them.'

★ ★ ★

When she returned to the coffee lounge, Luke and Nell were sharing a joke and she watched them unobserved for a few moments.

Nell was smiling up at him now, catching at his sleeve and listening intently to something he was saying.

Lydia could see that he was enjoying the girl's company, too. She felt a sharp stab of envy at their easy rapport and was ashamed of herself for minding so much.

She crossed the room to join them and fortunately, shortly afterwards, Nell announced she needed to go.

'Sorry about that,' Luke said.

Lydia looked at him in surprise. 'What exactly are you apologising for?'

'It seems that our evening has been hijacked by Nell.'

'That's fine by me,' she told him.

'She's so full of vitality, isn't she? I'm surprised you didn't photograph her.'

'That's Trent's province. He's going to do that portfolio for her — remember?'

'Of course,' Luke said, and there was an odd expression on his face. Perhaps he really was keen on Nell, she decided with a sinking feeling.

* * *

Shortly afterwards, they left the hotel and made their way back to Hill House. Jenny had obviously been listening out for the car.

'There's been a telephone call for you, Luke — someone called Simone. She tried ringing Willow Cottage and then your mobile, but didn't get any answer.'

'That's because I switched it off in the dining-room and forgot to switch it back on. Anyway, the signals are so poor up here, aren't they? Thanks,

172

Jenny, I'll get back to her.' And, with a nod, he drove off into the night.

'She sounded as if it was quite urgent,' Lydia's sister told her. 'Oh, dear, perhaps I ought to have phoned the hotel, but I thought you'd be back before this — was it a good evening?'

'It might have been — if Nell hadn't decided to show up.'

Jenny looked frankly astounded. 'Nell! She really is the limit! Admittedly I mentioned where you'd gone, but I'd no idea she'd barge in. Come on, we'll have a nightcap and you can tell me all about it.'

Lydia was glad to turn the conversation away from Luke's phone call. Who was Simone? she wondered, her mind working overtime.

She might have known there would be someone in his life.

An Engagement Is Announced

As they sat enjoying a glass of wine and watching a late night movie, Jenny said, 'Lydia, Mum rang while you were out, too.'

Something in her tone made Lydia look at her sister sharply.

'Nothing's wrong is it? How are Carole and the baby?'

'They're fine — stop worrying. It's just that, well, I think you may be right about there being some reason why Luke isn't too keen on the relationship that's developing between Aunt Mattie and Joel.'

'How d'you mean — what did Mum say?'

'Nothing much — it's just the way she said it. You know, all mysterious as if there was a secret.'

'Exactly like you're being now . . . come on spill, Jenny! The suspense is killing me!'

'Well, I thought I'd just ask her if she knew of any reason why Luke might be against his uncle being so chummy with Aunt Mattie, and she said — ' Jenny paused to take a sip of wine, leaving her exasperated sister staring at her. 'She said that perhaps there was something — something that happened a long time ago.'

'To do with Aunt Mattie and Uncle Ted?'

'She wouldn't say — just that we could ask Dad, but it's probably best not to drag up the past.'

Lydia stared blankly at the TV screen for a moment or two. Luke had said something . . . Suddenly, she put down her glass and snapped her fingers. 'Luke said something about the current trend for looking into family backgrounds, and it not always being a good idea. I wonder if he was hinting at something.'

'It might have just been an idle,

unrelated comment,' Jenny suggested.

'Oh, come on, Jen — it doesn't take a genius to work out that he's opposed to the relationship that's developed between his uncle and Aunt Mattie.'

'I don't actually understand what *you've* got against it, Lyddie. If it's just the money thing, then that's surely up to them and if not, then what's the problem?'

Lydia stared at her sister. 'You just don't get it do you? What if he asks her to marry him? Apart from Janet, Mattie has no blood relations and so we've got to look out for her. Uncle Ted would have wanted that. She was devoted to him and he to her.'

'But surely that doesn't mean she can't enjoy the friendship of another man?'

'But Joel seems to want to change everything, Jen.'

'Bring everything into the twenty-first century you mean,' Jenny said, in her down-to-earth way. 'Well, is that so very bad? If the attic conversion is

176

anything to go by then, personally, I'm all for it. Anyway, who said anything about them getting married?'

Lydia could see that she wasn't going to get anywhere by pursuing the subject. She got to her feet, 'Fancy a hot drink?' she asked and went into the kitchen to put the kettle on.

★　★　★

As soon as breakfast was over the following morning, Jenny set off with Maisie to spend the morning with Nell and her friends. Luke was nowhere to be seen and, as it was Gemma's day off, Lydia and Mrs Dalton had to work extra hard to get the chores done. A couple of the guests had moved out and had left their room in rather a state, and an indescribable mess in the bathroom.

'Luke is a proper gentleman,' Mrs Dalton observed as she tackled the bath. 'He's just like his uncle — never a thing out of place and such good manners.'

'He comes from a big family,' Lydia said, 'I expect he's always had to do his share around the house.'

Mrs Dalton didn't look up from her task. 'Must be odd not knowing your mother. And I can't imagine what it must be like to know you weren't wanted. Mr Norris told me that Luke was brought up by his aunt and her husband.'

'Well, he's obviously got a lovely family. Did you see the photograph on Luke's bedside table when he was up in the attic?' Lydia asked casually.

Mrs Dalton picked up the bath cleanser again. 'This tub couldn't be worse if they'd bathed a sheep in it! What's that you were saying about a photograph, Lydia?'

Lydia repeated her question adding, 'They all looked so friendly.'

'Yes. Well, Mr Norris is a lovely gentleman too. I never thought Mrs Lawson would find anyone after her husband died. Mr Norris is very different from your Uncle Ted, but he sort of fits in, if you know what I mean.'

Prudently, Lydia decided not to pursue the matter any further for the time being but, suddenly, the older woman said, 'You've just reminded me, Lydia, talking about family photos. We got rid of a lot of things in the attic, but your aunt particularly asked me to put the photograph albums and letters out of harm's way. Until now, I'd completely forgotten about them — what with all the upheaval during the past few months — and I bet she has too.'

'So where are they then?' Lydia asked.

Mrs Dalton set down the bath cleanser, and eased her aching back.

'I think they're in the laundry cupboard, at the back of one of the shelves. I'll look them out for you when I've got a moment.'

* ★ *

Jenny and Maisie had enjoyed their morning. 'It was great in the juicy,'

Maisie told Lydia. 'Nell's friends are fun — Rob tells lots of jokes.'

'Good job she didn't understand them,' Jenny murmured. 'Rob hasn't a clue about kids, but Maisie's used to being with adults so she occupies herself and, to give him his due, he did let her have a go on his computer for a little while.'

The three of them spent the afternoon having a nice leisurely stroll by Lake Ullswater, getting back in time for tea.

Afterwards, Lydia deliberated over what she ought to wear that evening and finally decided on the only dress she had brought with her. It was in a pretty shade of green with a lowish neckline which showed off her curves. Jenny did her hair for her, sweeping it up high, and she applied the merest hint of make-up — just eyeliner and a slick of lip gloss.

'Wow!' Luke said admiringly when he arrived. 'Can I take Cinderella to the ball?'

She grinned. 'I thought I'd better

prove that I can make the effort sometimes. You look pretty good yourself.'

He was attired in dark blue trousers and a lighter jacket with a pale blue, open-necked shirt.

'Thank you, kind lady. I suppose if I return you after midnight, you'll turn into a pumpkin?'

Maisie chuckled. 'I'd like to see that. You could make her into a pumpkin pie, Uncle Luke.'

'What a waste,' he said quietly and, just for a split second, Lydia felt a warm glow, even though she realised he was probably an expert at flattery and didn't mean a word of it.

'I believe you'll find it was the coach that changed back into a pumpkin — not Cinderella, Maisie, so I'd just turn into Mrs Mop again,' she said lightly.

★ ★ ★

The house, which belonged to Rob's mother, was beautiful and, much to

Lydia's surprise, she found herself enjoying the evening.

Trudi and Rob were a lively couple, and good company.

Rob was a scruffy, jeans-clad young man but Trudi, a rather giddy red-head, was wearing an amazing lime-green top with white cropped trousers underneath, and Nell was her usual, sophisticated self in a skimpy black dress that showed off her long legs to advantage. Beside them, Lydia felt about a hundred.

Presently, a couple more of their friends arrived and the music got rather loud.

'What is it you do, Rob?' Lydia asked above the din.

He grinned wryly. 'I'm an artist, but it's difficult to make much money so I have to diversify a bit.'

'He works in a supermarket to bring in a bit of cash,' Trudi chipped in. 'I'm into fashion. Nell tells me Trent is going to do a portfolio of her. I've always told her she'd make a great model.'

'I thought you all trained together,' Lydia said, trying to make sense of this.

'We were all at university together but we took different courses. Anyway, most people seem to end up doing something totally different from what they set out to do. There's so much competition. You're lucky finding something you really like, Lydia, and being able to make a go of it.'

'Yes, I suppose I am,' she replied. 'I ought to count my blessings.'

'That sounds profound,' said Luke, looking at her with a smile.

Nell was sitting close beside him and she gave a little laugh. 'Lydia's too serious for her own good. She has all these deep thoughts.'

'Needs to lighten up, does she?' asked Rob and, catching Lydia by the hand, pulled her protestingly to her feet and into a crazy dance, until breathless and laughing she sank back on to the sofa. She was aware that Luke was looking at her, faintly amused.

'You see,' he said, 'she's got hidden depths!'

After that, Rob danced with Trudi, and Nell whispered something to Luke so that he took her hand and led her on to the floor.

She quite provocatively pressed herself closer to Luke than was necessary, but when the music changed to a softer tempo, he came across to Lydia, held out his hand to her and pulled her to her feet.

She caught her breath as he took her in his arms, feeling the warmth emanating from his body and wondering if he was as aware of her as she was of him. She was also aware that the others were watching as she matched her steps to his.

All too soon, the moment was over and they went back to their seats.

They left shortly after and, as they were driving back along the narrow roads, Luke said, 'You mustn't let Nell wind you up, Lydia. You're a sitting target.'

'I don't know what you're talking about,' she told him stiffly.

'Nell's young and hasn't acquired the art of tact. She has a wicked sense of humour and stunning good looks and knows exactly how to manipulate people.'

'Well, she doesn't manipulate me!'

He shot her a swift glance. 'Right — so that's why all the time she's been up here, she's done mainly what she's wanted and you've found yourself fitting in with her plans?'

She could think of nothing to say to this. She realised she must appear a gullible fool in his eyes. They drove along in silence for a time and then he said, 'I suppose your aunt and my uncle will be returning in a day or two. Judging from the e-mails and text messages I've received, they've had a thoroughly good time.'

'Yes. Jenny and I had a postcard from Aunt Mattie yesterday.'

'So are you staying on after their return?'

It was a casual enough question, but she suspected it was calculated.

'Just for a few days.'

She wanted to add that there was nothing for her to rush back to. Not now that she and Trent had split up. There was nothing waiting for her at home but a lot of heartache, hassle — and money worries, if Trent decided to pull out of the studio.

'So, what about you?' she asked now.

'Me? Oh, probably the same. By rights, I should be back at work by the end of the week, but I can wangle a few more days off, I guess.'

'Thanks for all your help,' she said, and knew that she meant it.

'It's been a pleasure and very interesting. And I've enjoyed meeting Mattie's family.'

And was that it? she wondered. She knew that she was going to miss Luke and would have liked to see more of him. Without realising it, he had helped her to make up her mind up about Trent, who she'd seen in a different light. She knew for certain now that she'd be happier with someone more mature — someone like Luke, she realised with a start.

She sat staring out of the car window as the shock of this revelation hit her. Jenny had always told her that one day — when she least expected it — her dream man would come along and, suddenly, she realised it was Luke and that if she wasn't careful she'd end up falling for him in a big way.

With a jolt, she remembered that he already had a girlfriend — the mysterious Simone who was probably like an older, more mature version of Nell.

Then she realised that they'd arrived back at Hill House and she snapped out of her reverie.

$\star$ $\star$ $\star$

It was Jenny's turn to go out on Thursday. She and Maisie had been invited to visit friends in Penrith who had a couple of children. Luke had kindly offered to help clear away after breakfast so that they could leave early.

The morning was hectic. But some of the guests had departed, including Mr Jones, who had stayed much longer than he'd originally intended, so — for the next day or two — with less rooms to clean, the workload wouldn't be so arduous.

Mrs Dalton had looked out the old photograph albums that morning and, as they sat out in the garden over welcome cups of coffee, Lydia said, 'Have you seen these albums, Luke?'

'No, what are they?'

'Old photographs of Uncle Ted's. I remember him showing them to us when we were small.'

She'd asked him, the previous evening, about the woman in the family group from his bedside table, and he'd said that she was his Aunt Mary, the woman who'd been like a mother to him when his real mum had abandoned him.

Flicking through one of the albums,

Lydia didn't really know what she was expecting to find but, as she turned the pages, she suddenly realised why she'd recognised the woman in Luke's family photo. There was a picture of her in Uncle Ted's album, arm linked through his, smiling up at him. Lydia shut the album with a snap.

'Thanks, Mrs D. I'll see that these are replaced in the attic cupboard.'

There was something going on here that she didn't understand. How was it that Uncle Ted had known Luke's Aunt Mary? With a start, she suddenly realised that, as Mary was Joel Norris' sister, it was more than likely he'd known the entire family. So what did it all mean?

'You're very quiet, Lydia,' Mrs Dalton said presently. 'Are you OK?'

She forced a smile. 'Absolutely — just a bit tired that's all. So, what's next on the agenda?'

★ ★ ★

As soon as Jenny returned from her outing, Lydia shared her news with her.

Jenny frowned. 'OK, I'll admit it's strange that neither Joel nor Aunt Mattie have ever mentioned that our families have met before — but there's probably a perfectly logical explanation. I mean, are you absolutely certain that it is Luke's aunt?'

For an answer, Lydia went up to the attic room and fetched the albums. The sisters pored over them for several minutes.

There was more than one photograph of the same woman. She was photographed with Uncle Ted in one picture, and in another with some people that neither of them recognised. 'It's a pity Luke's taken back his photograph from the bedside table. It's all a bit of a mystery, isn't it?'

'Don't go making too much of it, Lyddie. Best to let sleeping dogs lie, as Dad says, eh?'

Lydia, who was trying to make sense of things, frowned at her sister.

'I still don't understand why Aunt Mattie has never said that Joel's family knew Ted. I mean, what else hasn't she told us?'

'That she's related to the Queen of Sheba? Come on, leave well alone. If there's something Aunt Mattie wants to tell us, then she will, all in her own good time. She's a very straightforward sort of person.'

'That's always supposing that she actually knows about the connection herself.'

An idea popped into Lydia's head, one that she could hardly bring herself to express.

'Luke said he never knew his mother — that she didn't want anything to do with him. He also hinted that she'd been an unmarried mum . . . You don't suppose . . . ?'

Her mind was working overtime.

'If Uncle Ted was friendly with Luke's Aunt Mary . . . could there be a possibility that . . .'

Jenny had stopped what she was

doing and was staring at her sister, as if she could not believe what she was hearing.

'If you're hinting at what I think you are, Lyddie, then it's absolutely out of the question! You're surely not suggesting that Uncle Ted might have had an affair with Luke's mother?'

She nodded. 'I realise it sounds improbable but . . . '

'Luke's told you — his father died in a motorbike accident before he was born! You're letting your imagination run away with you, little sister.'

Lydia sighed. 'Yes, I'm sorry, it was a stupid thought!'

And a dreadful one, too, for if there was any truth in it then Luke, Jenny and herself would be cousins and that would be the very last thing she wanted.

'But why is Luke so opposed to Aunt Mattie's relationship with Joel?' she persisted.

Jenny looked exasperated. 'We've been over this ground before — same reason as you, I suspect. Afraid that they've got designs on each other's money!'

And Lydia reluctantly realised that, so far as her sister was concerned, the matter was closed. She took the albums upstairs again and returned them to the shelf in the attic cupboard.

★　★　★

Aunt Mattie and Joel returned at the end of the week, both looking relaxed — and Aunt Mattie looking about ten years younger. Her hair had been restyled and she was wearing an outfit in a shade of blue that brought out the colour of her eyes.

They'd only been back at Hill House for a few minutes before she said, 'We've got some news!' And she rather shyly stretched out her hand to show off an antique diamond ring.

'Your aunt has agreed to be my wife,' Joel Norris said gruffly.

There were hugs all round. Whatever

reservations Lydia and Luke might have had in private, it was obvious that their aunt and Luke's were sublimely happy.

With a muttered excuse, Luke disappeared, to return a short while later with a bottle of champagne.

'Can I be a bridesmaid?' Maisie wanted to know.

Aunt Mattie bent down to the child's level. 'If I was going to have a bridesmaid, you'd be the very first to be asked but, you see, it's going to be a very quiet wedding — just six of us.'

Maisie looked disappointed. 'Jodie's been a bridesmaid twice already and I wanted to tell her when I phoned that I was going to be one and now I can't even come to your wedding!'

'Never mind, darling, there'll be plenty of other opportunities for you to be a bridesmaid, I'm sure.'

Jenny took her small daughter to one side and tried to explain, finding it hard to accept, herself, that her aunt didn't want them at her wedding.

On Saturday evening, they had a special dinner which Aunt Mattie insisted on cooking herself. Jenny and Maisie were leaving for home early the next morning and, unexpectedly, Luke had said he'd have to leave, too.

Aunt Mattie was an excellent cook and the roast beef was delicious.

Joel was on form and kept them all amused with anecdotes about the cruise. He was a jolly little man with twinkling brown eyes and a ready smile, a bit like Luke's.

'So how did your comedy act go?' Lydia asked him.

For a moment he looked startled and then he said, 'Oh, I suppose Luke mentioned it, did he? I think it went well enough — what did you think, Mattie?'

'He was a triumph. The audience loved him,' she said, and there was a faraway look in her eyes.

Jenny, who hadn't a clue what they

195

were talking about, had to have it explained to her.

'Well, you are a dark horse,' she told Joel. 'Of course, Uncle Ted used to be on the comedy circuit, many years ago. You two would have had a lot in common.'

'Did you ever get to meet Uncle Ted?' Lydia asked suddenly, watching his face carefully.

Before Joel could reply, Luke sprang to his feet. 'I'm really sorry to break up the party, but I've just remembered that I've got a couple of phone calls to make. Thanks for everything, Mrs Lawson. I'll pop in tomorrow to say goodbye before I leave.'

'You'd better!' Aunt Mattie told him.

'If you're ringing Simone, say 'hello' to her from me,' his Uncle Joel told him.

Later on, Lydia, fully aware of how Luke had deliberately changed the subject, mentioned it to Jenny who had popped into her room for a chat before bed.

'Do you think it's possible that Joel could have known Uncle Ted? Is that what all this is about? Perhaps the two of them didn't get on or something?'

Jenny looked thoughtful. 'It's probably just that Luke remembered the phone calls. After all, why wouldn't Joel want us to know if he had met Uncle Ted? In any case, it would have been years ago. Uncle Ted gave up treading the boards when we were still quite young. We only know so much about it because of all those photographs he used to show us . . . ' She trailed off and looked at Lydia. 'There was another album, wasn't there?' she said slowly. 'One in which there were loads of pictures of him in costume. I wonder what happened to it?'

Remembering, Lydia nodded. 'So, now do you see? There is something, isn't there? I bet Luke wishes he hadn't mentioned about his Uncle Joel having been a comedian.'

'It was bound to come out sooner or later,' Jenny said.

'And what's all this about them wanting a quiet wedding? Aunt Mattie loves a party.'

'I agree it's a bit out of character but, perhaps, when you get to their age . . .'

'But we're family,' Lydia protested. 'Mum and Dad will be so hurt, and what about Aunt Janet?'

'Perhaps she'll be invited. After all, Aunt Mattie did say there were to be six at the wedding. Now, on a totally different tack — who's Simone?'

Lydia shook her head. 'Search me — presumably Luke's lady friend. You took the call when she rang up the other day, Jen. What did she sound like?'

'Slightly put out that she couldn't contact him. Oh, well, I supposed it was only to be expected that he'd have a girlfriend.'

★ ★ ★

The next day, after Jenny, Maisie and Luke had departed, the house seemed empty, even though there were a number of guests staying as usual. Lydia would be leaving the following day, but felt it would have been wrong for everyone to go at once.

'You're looking a bit pale, dear,' Aunt Mattie told her niece as she helped with the round of domestic chores. 'This hasn't been much of a break for you, has it? You've been rushed off your feet.'

'I've enjoyed it — I needed a bit of space to sort myself out,' Lydia assured her aunt.

'Darling, you can tell me! It's Trent, isn't it? Jenny let something slip.'

She nodded miserably and told Aunt Mattie what had happened.

'Lydia, he's not worth it! I know I haven't met him, but from what you've told me, you need to think very carefully before getting yourself into a situation you might regret.'

'I already have,' she told her aunt. 'Trent and I are history. I've been very naïve. It seems he's been using me all along. The problem is what to do if he pulls out of the studio.' Her eyes filled with tears. 'A month ago everything was going fine. And now it's all changed.'

Her aunt gave her a reassuring hug. 'Life's like that, darling. It'll all come right, you'll see. After all, who would have thought I'd have found happiness again at my age?'

Lydia gave a weak smile, but her aunt couldn't and mustn't know, either about her niece's reservations concerning her engagement to Joel — or that she was attracted to Luke.

A Wedding Invitation

Lydia had been dreading returning to Canterbury, but things there went better than expected. For much of the week she saw very little of Trent. Somehow they contrived to keep out of each other's way. There were no school engagements and he coped with their only wedding appointment single-handed. When their paths crossed, they were coldly polite to one another and, in front of the clients, civil enough.

She was glad to be able to throw herself into her work for it gave her very little time to think. She knew that both she and Trent were playing for time and that, eventually, they would have to discuss the situation. She missed the easy-going relationship she had previously enjoyed with him, and their friendship too.

She had other things on her mind,

however, to keep her occupied.

As they had enjoyed a quiet supper on the evening before her departure from Hill House, Lydia had asked her aunt about the missing photograph album. For an answer, Aunt Mattie had gone to the wall unit and produced it with a smile.

'Some of my favourites are in this one,' she had told Lydia. She had left her niece flicking through the album, while she had gone off to attend to one of her guests who needed a plaster for a blister.

Although Lydia had seen the photographs many times before, she had looked at them with renewed interest and, as she reached the back of the album, she came across two blank pages. It was evident from the faded paper that some photographs had been removed. Joel had turned up at that point and Lydia had decided not to ask Aunt Mattie about the missing photographs in front of him.

When she rang her mother, after her return to Canterbury, Lydia was promptly asked to lunch that coming Sunday. Mrs Lawson then went on to say, 'Actually, I was speaking to Marcia the other day — just to find out how she was after her accident. She was over the moon because Nell has been taken out to dinner by that nephew of Joel's — Luke, is he called? I understand he's in hotel management. Apparently the hotel he's based in, in Kensington, is very swish and very expensive. Nell raved about it.'

Lydia's heart plummeted. How typical of Nell. She only had to flutter her eyelashes and men came running.

'Are you all right, dear?' her mother's voice came from the other end of the line. 'I suppose you didn't get much time to yourself while you were in Silverdale. Mind you it was nice that Trent was able to get up for a weekend, wasn't it?'

Lydia hadn't yet told her mother that she and Trent were no longer an item, and she certainly couldn't face being cross-examined about the reason — that he'd wanted to move in with her. Her parents were quite conventional and her mother, in particular, had never really taken to Trent. So Lydia said carefully, 'Yes. But, of course, I had Maisie and the guesthouse to look after, so we didn't spend too much time together. Anyway, I don't think it was his scene.'

'Really? I would have thought that, being a photographer, he would have found plenty to keep him occupied, even if you couldn't be with him every minute of the day.'

'Oh, he'd already been to an exhibition in Manchester and he doesn't want to eat, breathe and sleep photography any more than I do,' she said rather irritably.

'Isn't the business going too well, dear?' her mother enquired.

Lydia was tempted to tell her that Trent was threatening to move out of the premises, but something made her withhold this piece of information.

'Oh, it's going well enough, but digital photography is likely to put the kibosh on a lot of small businesses like ours and, although it has its place and Trent is a convert, we both refuse to give up the more traditional methods.'

It was a subject on which they agreed in the main.

'People just seem to think they can take a snapshot on their mobile phone and mess about on the computer — which is all very clever in its own way, but real photography is an art form in its own right.'

'Yes, dear,' her mother said. 'Anyway, you're preaching to the converted here!'

She wisely changed the subject, telling Lydia about her brother, Andrew, and the new baby.

★ ★ ★

On Friday afternoon, Lydia was looking forward to a quiet weekend, when the door to the studio opened and Nell stood there, looking bewitchingly lovely in a pale-pink dress, her make-up perfect and her hair like molten gold as the sun caught it.

Beside her, Lydia felt hot, tired and a frump.

'Nell, what a surprise! I didn't know you were coming ... is everything OK?'

Nell looked startled. 'I've come for the photo shoot. Could you let Trent know I'm here. He's expecting me.'

So that was it! How could Lydia have forgotten? She forced a smile.

'He's with a client at the moment — would you like a coffee?'

Nell selected a seat in the waiting area. 'No thanks.'

Lydia noticed that she had a small overnight bag with her. 'Are you planning on staying over?'

'What? Oh no — I've just brought a few things to change into for the shoot, and then Trent's taking me out to dinner.' She saw Lydia's expression and added, as an afterthought, 'Jenny told me you two had split up — that is right, isn't it?'

Lydia swallowed, thinking that the other girl hadn't wasted any time.

'Well, yes — but I'd heard that you'd been seeing Luke. Or at least, that you'd been out to dinner with him last week.'

Nell looked faintly taken aback. 'How news travels!'

'Yes, doesn't it? Your mother told my mother. It seems Marcia was full of it. Thinks it's the best thing that's happened to you for a long time.'

Nell tossed back her mass of blonde hair. 'Right, so, don't disillusion her if you speak to her, will you? You see, I know she'd disapprove of this and I don't want her finding out.'

'About the photo shoot or you having dinner with Trent?' Lydia asked wickedly.

A slight smile played about Nell's

lips. 'Both, actually. She likes the idea of my dating an older, more mature man like Luke.'

'And what about you? Or do you just enjoy being wined and dined?'

Nell looked slightly uncomfortable. 'I think Luke's too old for me, to be honest. And I prefer Trent's company. He's more fun. He came up to see me in London last weekend. I'm surprised he didn't tell you.'

Lydia caught her breath.

'Anyway, Luke is obviously very involved with Simone and I wouldn't want to share him.'

'So did Simone have dinner with you, too?' Lydia found herself asking.

Nell gave a little laugh. 'No, of course not!' She flicked back her hair. 'Luke's hotel is really swish and the food was divine!'

Lydia mumbled a reply and was relieved when, a few minutes later, Trent appeared in the doorway of his studio.

'Nell, how lovely to see you! Come on in.'

He pointedly ignored Lydia, and she busied herself in her studio, trying to ignore the sound of muffled laughter coming from the other side of the wall. It was no good being jealous. Her relationship with Trent had ended abruptly and painfully, and she had to accept that it really was over. He wasn't wasting any time in moving on, and this made her realise that his feelings for her couldn't have been as deep as he had pretended.

She brushed away a tear, realising that her pride was hurt.

Shortly afterwards, she locked her studio and went upstairs to her flat where she poured herself a glass of wine as she cooked her solitary supper and listened to the radio. Perhaps she should get herself a cat. At least it would be company during the long evenings! First Luke and now Trent had dated Nell. She remembered Nell's remark about Simone and wondered why Luke had asked Nell to dinner when he was still very evidently involved with someone else.

She decided it had probably never even entered his head that Nell would have any romantic designs on him. He was just a thoroughly nice man who, no doubt, thought of Nell like a younger sister.

★ ★ ★

Saturday passed pleasantly enough for Lydia. She visited some friends who insisted she stayed for dinner. When she went to see her parents on Sunday, her mother wanted to know all about her trip to the Lakes and, of course, all about Joel and Mattie's engagement.

'You haven't said much about Joel's nephew. Jenny says he stayed at Hill House and made himself useful, and Nell obviously enjoys his company — so what's he like?'

'Oh, he's OK — he works in a hotel in London, as you know,' she replied casually.

As Lydia thought of Luke, images of

him came into her mind. Luke who, with his rugged good looks, dark hair and eyes, had the power to set her pulse racing wildly.

She thought of him laughing as Maisie said something funny, of his captivating smile and muscular body, and the way she had felt when he'd danced with her. Her mother was staring at her — a concerned expression on her face.

'Are you all right, darling? You're very quiet and you don't seem your usual self.'

Lydia assured her mother that she was just a little tired.

'Well, you've obviously had a hectic time. Now, I'm just going to put the vegetables on and then we can have an early lunch. We're just having fruit salad for dessert. After all, if we're going to Carole and Andrew's for tea, then we'd better leave some room.'

Over lunch, they discussed Aunt Mattie's forthcoming wedding.

'I can't say I'm surprised that it's

going to be such a quiet affair,' Lydia's father commented, 'although, I must admit, I did think we'd have been invited but, as your mother's pointed out, it's a long way to travel and there are rather a number of relatives on Joel's side, so I suppose they decided it would have to be all or none.'

'Well, I still think it's a shame we won't be there,' Lydia said. 'Aunt Mattie only has Aunt Janet and us. And, I suppose, once she's married again, we won't really be family at all.'

Her mother frowned. 'I'd never really thought of it like that, dear, but I suppose you're right. Although, I can't see Mattie disowning us, can you?'

Lydia shook her head and her father looked thoughtful.

'Do you know who's making up the wedding party, Lyddie?' he asked now.

'Probably their local friends — shall I fetch the fruit salad?'

⋆ ⋆ ⋆

Over dessert, Lydia said tentatively, 'I was wondering — do either of you have any idea whether Joel Norris might have met Uncle Ted?'

There was a pause, and then her father said brightly, 'I think I'll just go and get the car out of the garage, ready for us to drive over to Andrew and Carole's.'

Lydia stared at his retreating back in surprise, then explained to her mother about the coincidence of both Uncle Ted and Joel Norris being comedians, and about the missing photographs.

'I don't suppose you happen to have any old snapshots of Uncle Ted, do you?'

Her mother began to clear the table. 'Probably only ones that you've seen many times before. I'll look them out, but there isn't time now. Is there any particular reason why you want to see them?'

'Just curiosity, I guess.'

* * *

Carole and Andrew's baby, William, was gorgeous. Lydia could have cuddled him the entire afternoon, but Carole had a strict routine and so, reluctantly, she put him down. She was, however, allowed to take a few photographs of him.

Although there were still things troubling her, Lydia felt more relaxed when they left.

It was still quite early when they arrived back at her parents' house and, after another coffee, she was preparing to set off for home when her mother handed her a package in a carrier bag.

'Just a fruit cake and a few scones — oh, and I found that album you were asking about. It belonged to your granny — your Dad's mum. But don't mention it again in front of your father, dear. There are some things best left unsaid. It was all such a long time ago.'

Her father came in from the garage at that point. 'What are we talking about?' he wanted to know.

'Cakes,' his wife informed him. 'I did

a massive bake last week and have given Lydia a cake to take back with her.'

He chuckled. 'Well, just so long as you've saved something for my tea. I saw that lovely Victoria sandwich you took to Carole's.'

'Well, you won't go hungry, there's another fruit cake in the tin — when do you think we'll see you again, darling?'

Lydia kissed her mother. 'I'm pretty busy for the next week or two, but I'll give you a ring. Perhaps we can meet up?'

⋆ ⋆ ⋆

As soon as she got in, she put on the kettle and then sat with her feet up, drinking tea and flicking through the pages of the album.

Besides some more recent photographs taken by herself, there were a number that she hadn't seen before. Then she realised that there were photographs tucked behind others and carefully extracted them.

She gasped as she examined them.

As well as pictures of Joel Norris with Uncle Ted, there were several of the dark-haired woman whom she now knew to be Luke's Aunt Mary.

There was also a snapshot showing Aunt Mattie and Joel together — obviously taken many years ago.

She removed it from the album and flicked it over to see if there was a date, but there wasn't.

What did it all mean? Why had Aunt Mattie given Jenny and herself the distinct impression that she'd only known Joel since he'd moved to the Lake District when, actually, she must have known him for many years!

She picked up the phone to speak to Jenny, then changed her mind. There was something here that she didn't understand. Something that obviously her parents knew about and didn't want to disclose to their children.

Lydia's mother, who never liked secrets and deceit, had let her have the album, probably hoping that she would

216

draw her own conclusions.

She suddenly realised that perhaps that's what Luke had been hoping, too, when he'd left his family photograph for her to see on the bedside table in the attic at Hill House.

She turned back to the album. There were photos of Joel and Uncle Ted in stage clothes, and other happy pictures of a picnic and a wedding.

Peering more closely she realised it must have been the marriage of Mary and her husband Thomas — Luke's uncle.

She gasped again when she realised who the other people in the photograph were. A smiling Mattie was bridesmaid and Uncle Ted was there too. It looked as if he might have been the best man.

She studied the photograph again, searching for something — anything — that might provide a clue and make things clearer. It just didn't make sense.

As she closed the album an envelope fluttered on to the floor.

Inside were a couple more photographs and a note, written in rather spidery black handwriting — presumably to her paternal grandmother.

Enclosed are a couple of snapshots of happier days.
If only we could put the clock back!

She examined the pictures. One was a group photograph, taken outside a house she did not recognise. Uncle Ted was there, and Mattie and Aunt Janet, and a young man she thought might be Joel but then, looking at the names that had been written on the back of the photo, she saw that it was someone called Robert and realised that this must be Joel's brother — Luke's father.

The other photo was of a smiling Uncle Ted on a motorbike.

It was late, but she had to speak to Jenny.

Jenny was surprised to hear from her sister, but listened patiently and then, when Lydia had finished, said, 'Right, so we've established Mattie knew Joel years ago and that Uncle Ted was friendly with both Joel and his brother Robert. But people move on and part company.'

Lydia sighed impatiently. 'So why, if it didn't matter, did Aunt Mattie let us believe she'd only met Joel when he arrived in Silverdale. Why has she kept quiet about her and Uncle Ted's past association with him?'

'Search me,' Jenny said wearily. 'At the end of the day, whatever happened between them in the past is history, and we must just wish them well for the future.'

'And I for one might be prepared to do that, if it wasn't for Luke's attitude. He's distinctly against their relationship and there has to be a reason,' she persisted. 'Besides, what do you think was meant by the reference in the letter to 'happier days'? What does any of it mean?'

'I've no idea, Lyddie, but if they want to tell us, then they'll do so in their own good time. Until then, let's just be glad that Mattie's found happiness all over again.'

As Lydia gathered up the photographs, she wondered if it was that simple. Why was she so concerned about something that had happened so long ago? Deep down, she knew it was because Luke Carstairs meant a great deal more to her than she cared to admit.

He'd made a lasting impression on her and she found herself thinking about him more than anyone must ever know.

★ ★ ★

On Monday, Trent was late arriving for work at the studio. Lydia was champing at the bit, wondering what was keeping him. They were due at an infant school at ten o'clock and she wanted to be on time.

He eventually came in whistling and looking pleased with himself.

'Sorry. The traffic was heavy and I had to get Nell to the station first.'

She made no comment, but her mind was working overtime.

Trent gave a boyish laugh. 'Now, don't let your imagination run away with you! She stayed with Sasha — not that it's any of your business.'

Sasha was a friend of his who ran a modelling agency.

'Of course it isn't,' she said lightly. 'Right, we'd best get a move on or we'll be late and Miss Pritchard will stand us in the naughty corner!'

★   ★   ★

Photography sessions in infant schools were generally hectic and this one was the usual mayhem with lots of face pulling, tears and tantrums, or just blank refusals to cooperate.

Then, besides the camera-shy, there were the little darlings who were determined to be child models and wanted everyone to know.

After the individual portraits came the class photos, with mischief written all over the children's faces.

Usually, Lydia loved the work but, at the back of her mind was an image of Nell with Trent. She couldn't help feeling a tiny bit hurt, but told herself she'd no right to be. She reminded herself it was all over between Trent and herself, so why should she care?

★ ★ ★

The rest of the week proved tiresome. It was incredibly busy, which Lydia didn't mind, but Trent announced that he was going to London on Wednesday and wouldn't be back until Thursday afternoon. He didn't tell her why and, because they no longer had the close relationship they used to, she didn't bother asking. After all, she'd had plenty of time off recently so she couldn't complain.

On Thursday evening, she'd just finished her dinner when the phone rang. To her surprise it was Aunt Mattie.

'I wanted you to be the first to know that I've fixed the date for the wedding — depending on whether . . . Lydia, I know it's a lot to ask, but could you do me a very big favour?'

'I'll do my best. What is it?' Lydia asked curiously.

'We could get married at the end of June — the vicar's had a cancellation but, of course, there's the guesthouse to consider and, although we can put off going away on a proper honeymoon until the autumn, we would like to have a few days to ourselves, so . . . '

'You were wondering if I'd cover for you?' Lydia finished for her. 'Well, of course I will. I'll just need to reorganise my schedule and pass on one or two appointments to Trent.'

'So, he's still around? I didn't like to ask.'

Lydia filled in her aunt with what had been happening and then asked, 'So when are you going away — on the day itself or the following morning?'

'On the evening we get married — just to Yorkshire. That way we can call in on your Aunt Janet.'

'She's not coming to the wedding then?'

There was a slight pause and then Aunt Mattie said, 'No, dear. We've discussed it and think it would be better all around if she came to stay later in the year, as usual, when we're around to entertain her. Besides, I said it was to be a quiet affair and it is — but Luke will be there, and so will you, darling, won't you?'

Lydia's heart practically missed a beat. Luke was to be there! She wondered who the other guests would be, but then Aunt Mattie said, 'Bridget and Patrick from the hotel are our other guests — just a simple affair. They've got friends who'll stand in for them at the hotel and Ginny and Jim will hold the fort here so that we can all go out for a meal after the ceremony.'

No sooner had Lydia put down the

phone than it rang again. This time it was Luke.

'Uncle Joel's just rung to invite me to the wedding and to ask if I could give you a hand again, running the guesthouse for a few days. He got your phone number from Mattie and passed it on to me — hope you don't mind?'

'Of course not — can you make it?' she asked carefully, trying not to sound too eager.

'Yes, if I juggle a few things around — meetings etc. How are things with you?'

They talked generally for a few minutes and then he said, 'Actually, I'm going to be in Canterbury next Wednesday. I've got a bit of business to do in the morning, but perhaps we could meet up for a meal in the evening?'

She caught her breath, but then she realised he probably only wanted to discuss arrangements for their trip to the Lakes. Suddenly, she wished she'd made some excuse to Aunt Mattie

— told her she couldn't manage it, after all, but she knew she had to put her own personal feelings on hold for the time being.

★ ★ ★

On Friday morning, Trent appeared with Nell. He sent her into his studio and leaned over the desk to talk to Lydia.

'Nell's been having a dreadful time at work. Her present job's really dull, so I suggested she came to work here. Sasha's got a few contacts in the modelling world, as you know, and it's what Nell really wants to do. So, while she's waiting for her big break, she can take care of reception here.'

'Since when have we taken on new staff without discussing it first?' Lydia demanded, endeavouring to keep control of her temper.

He gave a little laugh. 'We're not actually discussing much at all these days, are we? Anyway, for once I

226

thought you'd be pleased. She is a relative of yours, isn't she?'

'Nell had a perfectly good job in London, and a flat subsidised by her mother. You've managed to turn her head and make her believe she's going to become a model. Well, that just doesn't happen overnight, does it? Where's she going to live and what is she supposed to live on, may I ask? We can't afford to pay her much.'

Trent stared at her. 'Don't be such a wet blanket, Lydia! Oh, and I'd better give you warning. My friends in Ashford have asked me to join them in their business and I'm considering it. So it could be that you need to start looking for a new business partner!'

Lydia couldn't think of any quick reply to this and told him brusquely that he'd better look at his contract, as he'd need to give her time to find someone else, and then went into her studio and closed the door.

★ ★ ★

She was so angry that, as soon as she returned to the flat that evening, she picked up the phone to call Anthea, who was more than a little sympathetic.

'Is there any chance he'll change his mind?'

'No, I shouldn't imagine so. He seems to have it all worked out.'

'From what you're telling me, I'd have thought you'd have been relieved to see the back of him. He's treating you in a pretty shabby fashion, isn't he?'

'Yes. I think I've had a lucky escape.'

'Well, remember, if you decide to lease out the entire premises and make a fresh start, then come to me. You know I'd welcome you with open arms.'

'Thanks, Anthea, I know I can always depend on you. I've got quite a lot of serious thinking to do first, though.'

Lydia then went on to tell her about the wedding and Luke, but decided not to mention anything about their family affairs for the time being.

'Oh, good! So you two will be

coming up here again — and Lydia, don't let this one slip away. He's gorgeous!'

'He's already seeing someone,' Lydia told her, trying to sound matter-of-fact.

'Oh, that's a pity!' Anthea sounded as disappointed as Lydia felt. 'Anyway, I think Trent's a creep. I can say that now that you've broken up with him! I'm only thankful you didn't let him move in with you. He should have respected you for that and been prepared to give you more time. A bit of a control freak, is he?'

'I suppose he must be,' Lydia admitted, 'although it's taken me a long time to realise it. In fact he took me for a complete fool, and now I just hope he's not planning to treat Nell the same way.'

'From what you've told me about Nell, she seems quite capable of looking after herself.'

And Lydia had to concede that her friend was probably right. She realised she would have to resign herself to getting used to seeing Nell going about the place and out and about with Trent. She was also going to have to tell her mother about her break-up with Trent before someone else did.

* ⋆ ⋆

Surprisingly, Nell proved to be a very efficient receptionist and an absolute hit with the clients. She had a bubbly, effervescent personality and she was certainly doing her best to impress Trent.

On Wednesday, he had taken her out for an early lunch — in order to run through a few aspects of the job, he informed Lydia, who spent her lunch break catching up with her accounts — until the shop doorbell rang and she looked up to see Luke standing in the doorway.

Return To Silverdale

'I know we arranged to meet this evening, but I thought if you hadn't had lunch, perhaps you could keep me company.'

'I've got a family booked in for a group portrait at one-thirty, but after that, nothing more until three, so we'd have time for a sandwich. Look, why don't you get yourself a coffee and wait in here? Unless . . . you could always sit in, providing you promise to take a back seat.' Lydia tried not to sound too eager.

'Don't worry, I'll keep out of your way.'

She had time to give him a whistle-stop tour of the studios and was just showing him round the reception area when Nell and Trent came back.

'Are you still slaving away, Lydia? You really are a workaholic,' Nell said, and then, as she became aware of Luke studying some photographs in the small exhibition area, she cried, 'Luke, what are you doing here?'

He gave her a cool smile. 'Hello, Nell. Your friends told me you'd changed your job.'

Lydia saw the colour flood the other girl's face. 'As I told you, it was a bit of a dead-end job. This is far more exciting and fulfilling.'

'Well, you've only been here for a few days,' Lydia couldn't help pointing out. She wondered why Luke had wanted to contact Nell.

'I had a couple of complimentary theatre tickets I couldn't use, and thought of you,' he went on. 'Anyway, two of your friends soon snapped them up. Why are you here? I thought you were a city girl.'

'Canterbury is a city,' she told him defensively. 'Anyway, I can go to London whenever I choose, and stay over with my friends.'

'Yes, but it might be a tight fit — they

232

said to tell you your room is re-let to the girl who's taken your place at the office!'

Nell's face was a picture, and Trent — with a cool nod in Luke's direction — swept her into his studio.

'I just hope that young lady knows what she's doing,' Luke commented.

When Lydia's clients arrived, he sat watching her at work as she put the young family at their ease, gradually getting them into the relaxed, natural pose that she wanted.

'I'm afraid that took rather longer than I expected,' she said apologetically, as they ate a quick lunch at a café near the studio.

'I enjoyed watching you. I admire your skill. Err . . . I take it you and Trent are history — just colleagues nowadays?'

Lydia swallowed, suddenly feeling vulnerable and rather foolish.

'Who told you?'

'I'd drawn my own conclusions from what Nell's flatmates said.'

'We broke up in the Lakes — but it wasn't anything to do with Nell,' she said quietly, and found herself telling him that Trent was thinking of moving away to join forces with some friends.

He rubbed his chin. 'I see — and would he take Nell with him, do you suppose?'

'I really can't answer that. Their relationship has hardly got off the ground.' She crumbled the baguette on her plate and, not looking at him said, 'Anyway, I'm sure she enjoyed going out to dinner with you.'

He laughed. 'What Nell enjoyed was getting a free meal. She also turned up with Trent for coffee last week. I think she views me as a benevolent uncle.'

She registered relief and longed to ask him if his girlfriend, Simone, had objected to Nell turning up for freebies, but thought better of it. Instead, she brought up the subject of their forthcoming trip to the Lakes.

'Actually,' he told her, 'that's what I wanted to discuss. I thought we could both go up in my car — it seems a bit daft taking two.'

Once they'd sorted out their travelling arrangements, she finished her cappuccino and got to her feet.

'Sorry, but I'll have to get back now. Thanks for lunch.'

He stood up beside her. 'I'll see you again for dinner, then? Pick you up around seven?'

⋆ ⋆ ⋆

The last session ran a little late, but at long last Lydia escaped to her flat, desperate for a shower. Her black dress would have to do, she decided. There was no time to look out anything else. It was rather plain, but she had a silver bolero that would make it look more interesting. She swept up her hair, securing it with a comb and applied her make-up carefully.

She was just about ready when Luke arrived — looking amazingly handsome in an indigo blue shirt and dark suit. As she picked up her jacket, she was aware of him studying her appreciatively.

'I'm afraid my wardrobe doesn't cater for swish hotels,' she told him.

'You're looking lovely,' he reassured her, smiling.

It was a wonderful meal and he was great company, but all the time she felt the occasion was over-shadowed by thoughts of the unknown Simone.

As they sat over coffee in the lounge, she realised how aware she was of him. As he passed the cream, his fingers brushed hers and it was as if she had received an electric charge. She took a grip of herself.

'Luke, I know we've both got reservations about this wedding, but for Aunt Mattie and Joel's sakes we must try to be happy for them. I think we should both feel privileged that we've been invited.'

A shadow crossed his face. 'Are you actually aware of anything that might have happened to make me have reservations?'

'No, but I do know now that Aunt Mattie and Uncle Joel met years ago, because I've seen photographs that my mother showed to me — ones of your aunt and uncle's wedding, at which Mattie appears to have been a bridesmaid and Uncle Ted the best man.'

Luke's ears were slightly red, as if he was angry, she thought.

'What happened doesn't matter. There was a lot of bad feeling at the time, but it was all a long time ago, and now that your Uncle Ted is dead, these things should be buried with him.'

'Uncle Ted and Joel were friends once, weren't they?' she persisted, determined to get to the truth. 'How did they meet? Did they work together?'

'Look, Lydia, just leave it, OK? All you need to know is that your Uncle Ted ruined several people's lives.'

She stared at him. 'I don't know what all this is about, Luke. I truly have no idea.'

'And I have more idea than I ought,' he said, stirring his coffee vigorously. 'Look, all I'll say is that many years ago all our families were linked — yours, mine and Mattie's, but something happened to change all that — which is why . . . ' he trailed off as a hovering waiter came to offer more coffee, and the moment was gone.

He seemed so hurt and angry that for a mad moment, she wanted to catch hold of him, pull him to her and, somehow, make things better.

'Please, Luke, at least if you told me then perhaps . . . Whatever it was that happened, was it so very bad?' she asked gently.

His eyes clouded. 'Not for you, no — but, for me, it was devastating. Anyway, as I've told you before, it doesn't do to rake up the past. Now, can we please drop the subject?'

She nodded, realising that what had started out as an enjoyable evening had turned sour and it was all her fault. She should have known better than to confront him, but how else would she ever learn the truth when her own family seemed determined to cover it up?

* ★ ★

Luke drove her home practically in silence, but when they arrived at the studio, he insisted on seeing her to her flat.

When she thanked him for the evening he said, 'I hope we can still be friends, in spite of any differences our families might have.' And bending, he brushed her lips with his.

She stood there as his car pulled away, wondering if she had imagined the kiss, but knew from the way her heart was pounding that she hadn't. Then the cold harsh voice of reason spoke. Quite apart from any mysterious feud that might exist between their families, there was still Simone, lurking in the background.

★ ★ ★

For the next couple of weeks, Lydia didn't have time to brood, because she was kept busy with countless photographic sessions in schools, a couple of weddings, and a multitude of family portraits.

Then one afternoon she managed to find time to meet up with her mother, who'd come to Canterbury to buy a wedding present for Mattie and Joel.

They'd decided to go into a nice little coffee shop near the Cathedral for afternoon tea, and Lydia set about telling her mother that she'd split up from Trent.

'In the beginning, it was a bit of a shock,' Lydia admitted, 'but now I'm getting used to the way things are and I realise we just weren't right for one another.'

'Well, better you found out before it was too late, darling.' There was a pause and then her mother commented. 'Marcia seems pleased that Nell's moved to Canterbury. She thinks you'll be a steadying influence on her.'

Lydia nearly choked on her cake. 'Oh, Nell's very much her own person and not likely to take any notice of me,' she said, when she had recovered. She wasn't sure what Nell had told Marcia, and thought it wiser not to mention the modelling course for the present.

After a moment or two, her mother remarked, 'A pity nothing came of the friendship between her and Luke Carstairs, wasn't it?'

'He was much too old for her,' Lydia murmured into her cup.

'Oh, I rather think there was more to it than that. From what I can make out, there was someone else in the background. You got to know him quite well — did he ever mention a girlfriend?'

She shook her head. 'There were one or two phone calls from someone called Simone, but he never mentioned her to me.'

'So how do you feel about running the guesthouse with him again?'

'Well, it's only for a few days, isn't it? So it shouldn't be too arduous. Luke's a good cook and very competent, and we get on well enough.'

'Your father and I are naturally disappointed that Mattie didn't invite us to the wedding. We would have been happy to have helped out but, of course, if Janet isn't invited either . . .'

'I don't think it would have been appropriate in the circumstances, do you?' Lydia asked, watching her mother's face, but her expression gave nothing away.

'I don't think I follow what you're getting at, dear — what circumstances?'

'Mum, I realise that Joel and Uncle Ted were good friends at one time, and that Aunt Mattie obviously knew Joel from years back, but something happened, didn't it, to drive a wedge between our families and to make it awkward for us all to meet up.'

Her mother looked distinctly uncomfortable. 'All I can tell you is that Joel and Mattie were practically engaged at one time, but then your Uncle Ted met her and swept her off her feet and that was that!'

'That's hardly enough to cause a rift between the families, is it?' Lydia persisted. 'And those photos in the album are such happy ones, so something must have happened to change all that.'

Her mother picked up the bill.

'Well, perhaps there were one or two issues. Oh, it's all water under the bridge, now. Your father doesn't like dragging up the past. It upsets him, so I don't ask questions.'

It was obvious that her mother knew a great deal more than she was prepared to say and that Lydia was going to get precisely nowhere by questioning her. She reached for her jacket.

'Come on,' she said. 'Let's go and look for that wedding present.'

★ ★ ★

The next ten days flew by. It had been arranged that Luke would meet Lydia in Birmingham at Jenny's house so that they could both travel to the wedding in his car. She would leave her own car at her sister's and, after they'd had lunch with Jenny and Maisie, he would drive for the rest of the journey.

She made good time on the road from Canterbury to Birmingham, but, even so, Luke still managed to arrive before her.

She'd felt a bit apprehensive about seeing him again, but she needn't have worried, because he was his usual charming self and greeted her with a kiss on the cheek which sent her pulse racing.

Whatever happened, he mustn't suspect how she felt about him!

'I expect you've had to come away during a busy spell at the hotel,' she remarked.

'Oh, it's always busy, but my assistant manager is very capable. So, what have you been up to lately?'

She filled him in briefly and then Jenny came into the living-room with some coffee, followed a few minutes later by an excited Maisie, whose teacher had allowed her to have an extended lunch break.

Lunch was a happy affair but, almost

as soon as it was over, Lydia and Luke said their goodbyes and were on their way.

★   ★   ★

It was a smooth journey and, although there were one or two minor traffic hold-ups, they made good time so they were able to stop for refreshments en route, arriving at Hill House in time for an evening meal before Luke and Joel went off to Willow Cottage, leaving Aunt Mattie and Lydia to sit round the kitchen table with the remainder of a bottle of wine.

'I'm so glad you and Luke could make it, darling,' Mattie told her niece. 'I'd have liked all my favourite people to have been here, but we thought it best to keep it a small and simple affair. I just wonder what Ted would make of my marrying Joel? I do so hope he would be happy for me. I've not taken the decision lightly you know, Lyddie, in spite of what our families might think.'

Lydia, not knowing quite what to say, touched her aunt's hand. 'I'm sure Uncle Ted would want you to be happy and — well, he and Joel were friends once, weren't they? And you've known Joel for a long time, too, haven't you? Long before he came up here to live?'

There was a faraway expression on Mattie's face and Lydia waited with bated breath, wondering what — if anything — her aunt was about to tell her.

'Oh, yes, but you see, Joel was born and raised in Silverdale. I've known him since primary school — his family lived about three miles away from the village. He was a bit older than me, and once we went to our separate senior schools, I didn't see him again until one summer at a barn dance. We started going out together and I fell deeply in love with him. It was a magical summer and we thought it would go on forever but . . . ' She shook her head, as if to shake away the memories. 'You know, dear, I really fancy a nice cup of tea.'

Lydia made one last attempt to get to the bottom of the mystery.

'You were a bridesmaid at Joel's sister's wedding, weren't you? Uncle Ted was best man ... Mum came across the photo in an old album of my grandmother's.'

'My family had been friends with both Joel's and Ted's families for years.' Aunt Mattie said quietly.

'Right.' Lydia got up to put the kettle on and busied herself with the cups before asking casually, 'So, how come you married Uncle Ted and not Joel?'

'It was complicated. You see Joel and his family had to move to London. At first we kept in touch and he promised to visit, but time went by and we gradually drifted apart. Your Uncle Ted and Joel kept in touch though — their paths crossed in the theatre from time to time — but I didn't actually see Joel again until he looked me up recently, after your Uncle Ted died.'

Lydia handed her a cup of tea and fetched the biscuit tin.

'I always understood Uncle Ted came into the florist's shop one day and asked you out because he'd been stood up by someone else.'

Aunt Mattie smiled, 'Yes, that's more or less right. Your Uncle Ted had always had a soft spot for me, but it wasn't until Joel moved away from the area that he made his feelings plain. I don't think he would ever have married me if Joel hadn't left.'

Lydia wanted to ask why Joel had left, but thought better of it. None of this made any sense to her, but she supposed it was all to do with old fashioned principles and pride.

'So were you and Joel actually engaged before he went away?'

Aunt Mattie sipped her tea. 'No, but I think — or rather I know — that if things had been different . . . Don't get me wrong, dear, I loved your Uncle Ted and ours was a good marriage — although I had to put up with being without him from time to time when he went off on his tours. It was such a relief when he decided to give all that up a few years after we moved in here. Of course, we were never blessed with children but that was compensated for by the three of you. Anyway, all that seems a life-time ago and now I've got the future to look forward to with Joel.'

The Past Revealed

It was a perfect day for a wedding. Aunt Mattie looked amazing in an outfit of fuchsia pink with navy accessories. Her hat was a fabulous creation of feathers and frothy tulle. She looked years younger and Lydia was aware that any doubts she might have had concerning this marriage were unfounded.

Luke looked incredibly striking in a dark-grey suit with a pale-blue cravat.

Lydia was wearing a new dress in a misty-blue, floaty material.

'You look lovely,' Luke told her and she smiled up at him, feeling a warm glow of happiness within her.

It was a moving little service and the church was packed almost to overflowing with friends and well-wishers.

'So much for a quiet wedding,' Ginny murmured from the row behind.

After a magnificent meal in a nearby

hotel, the happy couple left for Yorkshire.

'That went well,' Luke said presently as he and Lydia sat in the little garden back at Hill House. 'I know we've both had our reservations but hopefully it'll all work out OK.'

'At first I thought they were on similar lines — our reservations, I mean. But now I realise I know nothing about whatever it is that's causing you concern, so don't you think we ought to get everything out in the open once and for all?' Lydia asked with great daring.

There was such a long pause that she thought she had really spoilt her chances of ever getting to the bottom of the family mystery, but then he said, 'All right, you go first — so what were your worries?'

He cupped his chin in his hands and watched her intently.

'Mine — oh, that's very straightfor-ward — I thought Joel had his eye to the main chance — you know, marrying a widow who was comfortably off.'

'You mean you thought he was after her money?'

She nodded and then demanded crossly, 'Why are you laughing?'

'Because Uncle Joel has more money than he knows what to do with! He's the one that's well off, Lydia!'

She suddenly felt rather foolish because wasn't that what Jenny had tried to tell her all along? 'I see — well, how — no, I mustn't ask!'

'No, that's OK, a wealthy widow on one of the cruise ships took a shine to him and left him all her money when she died . . . ' He burst out laughing at the expression on Lydia's face. 'Your face is an absolute picture! I just made that up! Actually, my grandmother was very well-off and all her children inherited quite a bit when she died fairly recently.'

'I see,' she said, trying to get her head round things. 'So what about your own reservations? Let me guess? You're under the impression that Aunt Mattie's a money-grasping widow?'

252

'I'll admit that, in the beginning, the thought did cross my mind but, actually, it's rather more complicated than that. It's a lengthy story and I've no intention of boring you with it all in one go but you're obviously aware now that Uncle Joel and your Uncle Ted were friends at one time?'

She nodded. 'The photographs told a story — so what happened? I know Uncle Ted was a bit of a lovable rogue from what my parents have told me about him over the years, but he was good to my brother, Jenny and myself, and I still think about him with affection.'

'I know you do, and I wouldn't want to change that but, you see, for me it's different. Your uncle was responsible for my father's death and I find that difficult to forgive!' Luke said harshly.

She looked at him blankly. 'I don't understand. You told me that your father was killed in a motorbike accident before you were born.'

Then she remembered something.

'There was a photograph that belonged to my grandmother of Uncle Ted on a motorbike.'

'Yes, probably the same motorbike that killed my father! Ted took my father — Robert — out on it for a ride one day. Your Uncle Ted was driving recklessly. My father was riding pillion without a crash helmet. Need I say more?'

Lydia shuddered. 'But you said it was an accident.'

'Yes, but Robert hated motorbikes. They frightened him. Ted laughed at him about it. Said he was being 'girly'. He was several years older than my father, and effectively bullied him into getting on to the back of that motorbike by making him feel he'd be a coward if he didn't. It was an irresponsible act that ruined several lives.' He sounded bitter.

'I can understand why you wouldn't have wanted to have anything to do with my uncle,' Lydia said at last, 'but he's dead now. And after all, what's

254

Aunt Mattie ever done to you?'

There was a bleak expression in his eyes. 'I have nothing personal against your aunt, Lydia, but you must see that this wedding brings back too many memories for my family. At one time, all of our families were on good terms but after what happened, and the consequences, who could blame them for not wanting any more to do with each other? Soon after the accident my family moved away from the village.'

'There's more, isn't there?' she asked, convinced that, even now, he hadn't told her everything.

'Yes, but it'll keep.'

They sat in silence for a few moments, deep in their own thoughts.

Eventually, Lydia said, 'My Uncle Ted was a lovely man. He was generous, warm-hearted, funny and now you're trying to make me think differently about him. Well, I'm sorry but I can't, Luke.'

He could have kicked himself for his insensitivity. He looked at her stricken face. His timing had been wrong. Quietly, he went into the house to return a few minutes later with two mugs of coffee. Placing one in front of her, he sat down again.

Lydia cupped her hands round her mug. 'I know you must have a very different opinion of my uncle, but if only you had known him.'

He sighed. 'We all perceive people differently, Lydia. I think of him as the man who took my father away from me.' He paused and then added quietly, 'And Mattie away from Uncle Joel.'

Her head shot up. 'You make it sound as if Aunt Mattie was the love of your uncle's life, but they were just teenagers when they knew each other before, and Uncle Ted and Aunt Mattie were always happy together.'

'Yes, I'm sure they were, but Ted took advantage of the fact that Joel was far away in London. Neither Mattie's parents nor my grandparents were keen for the relationship between her and Uncle Joel to continue after what happened — but I won't go into all of that. Joel told Mattie he'd come back to her, but Ted came along in his absence and began to take her out.'

'Well, she didn't have to go — she must have wanted to,' Lydia pointed out. 'She loved Uncle Ted,' she said stonily. 'And nothing you can say or do will make me think any differently.'

He reached out and took her hands between his. 'Lydia, you must believe me. I'm not trying to get you to change your feelings for your uncle. I've been prejudiced by my family against him, but I didn't know him.' He drained his coffee mug. 'Do you believe in love at first sight?'

She looked at him, startled. 'Well, yes, I suppose. Why?'

'I didn't — not until recently — but you see, my Uncle Joel never married because he never met anyone else who matched up to your aunt. He told me, not so long ago, that he loved her from the moment he first set eyes on her.'

She nodded, knowing that this was

something she would have to accept.

'I suppose it's possible to love two people at the same time, too.'

'They were very young,' he said, 'and, after what happened to my father, my grandparents tried to keep them apart. Joel thinks some of his letters might have been intercepted before they reached Mattie. When he turned up a couple of years later to find her, it was too late. She was already married to your Uncle Ted.'

Neither of them spoke for a while as they mulled all this over and then suddenly Lydia got to her feet. 'I'd better see if the guests are all right,' she said lamely.

When she returned to the kitchen, he was preparing a salad for their tea.

'I'm sorry,' he said presently as they enjoyed their simple meal.

'What for?' she asked dully. 'You can't be held responsible for the past.'

'No, but I am responsible for spoiling your day. I should have kept quiet until a more appropriate time.'

She shook her head. 'Yes, your timing could have been better but I suppose there wouldn't really have been a good time. I shan't change my mind though. I loved my Uncle Ted, warts and all, and I love Aunt Mattie too.'

'And I respect that but, if we're going to move on in our own relationship, then we have to bring everything into the open, don't we?'

She wondered what he was talking about.

'I've been honest with you all along and I'm hoping that from now on, Luke, you can be honest with me. I think there are still things you're not telling me. For a start, why should Joel's family want to keep him away from Aunt Mattie? What connection could she possibly have had with your father and his tragic death?'

'I think you've heard enough for now . . . There's a rather delectable fruit tart in the fridge,' he said, changing the subject.

'All you think about is food,' she

snapped at him.

'No, you're wrong there — quite often I think about you, Lydia.'

She stared at him, her heart beating a wild tattoo.

'Why would you do that?' she asked softly.

He made a move towards her and she caught her breath, her heart beating rapidly, but just as he took her hands between his, there was a knock at the door and one of the guests popped her head round.

'So sorry to trouble you, but the bulb's gone in my reading lamp and I was wondering if you could replace it?'

Luke sprang to his feet as if he couldn't wait to get out of the room and she wondered fleetingly what he had been about to say.

After that, two or three other minor problems cropped up, and then it was time to go through into the guests' sitting-room with the bottles of champagne and pieces of wedding cake that

Joel and Aunt Mattie had so thoughtfully provided. She didn't have another moment alone with Luke for the rest of the evening.

* * *

The following morning passed in a haze of breakfasts, bed-making and cleaning. Two of the guests left soon after ten o'clock and then, around mid-morning, another couple arrived to take their room.

In the afternoon, Mrs Dalton volunteered to be around so that Luke could accompany Lydia to the photographic exhibition in Keswick.

Anthea had managed to wangle a couple of hours off to accompany them, and was delighted to discover that she'd come first in the landscape class for her truly magnificent photograph of Derwentwater at sunset.

That was not the end of the surprises, however, for Lydia had also won a first prize for her photograph in the leisure section, of Maisie standing with twin lambs in the field near Hill House, with a wonderful view of the fells in the background. To her amazement, this had also been judged best exhibit in the show.

'I swore everyone to secrecy so that you could see for yourself. You are so talented, Lyddie — isn't she, Luke?' prompted Anthea.

'Absolutely!' he agreed.

In her delight, Lydia caught hold of his arm without thinking, and he gave her one of his special smiles, making her heart miss a beat.

'So what's the prize?' he asked.

'Oh, the photographs will be shown in a photographic magazine and, as best in the exhibition, Lydia gets a weekend for two in Rome with all expenses paid,' Anthea explained.

'And who will you take with you, Lydia?' His eyes surveyed her keenly so that she felt the colour rising to her cheeks. She mumbled something about one of her family and they went off to look at the rest of the exhibition.

'So, if Trent is no longer man of the moment then who will you take?' Anthea asked her friend as they paused to look at the same photograph.

Lydia gave a slight smile and shrugged, knowing whom she'd like to ask.

'How about Luke?' Anthea said. 'He's a lovely guy and I've got a sneaking suspicion you find him more than a little attractive.'

'Hush, Anthea!' But the tell-tale colour flooded her cheeks and she didn't deny it.

★ ★ ★

When they arrived back at Hill House, Gemma was hovering in the entrance hall.

'You've had a phone call, Luke. She rang a couple of times — it sounded urgent. You had your mobile switched off.'

He crossed to the desk and looked at

the scribbled number.

'Simone. Did she say what she wanted?'

Gemma shook her head. 'Only that you were to be told she'd rung the minute you returned.'

Lydia came back into the real world with a jolt. Just for a short while she had tried to imagine what it would be like if she and Luke could go to Rome together, but now she'd been abruptly reminded that Simone was still very much a part of his life.

★ ★ ★

The next couple of days were dull and drizzly and some of the guests opted to stay close to the guesthouse, so the eternal round of soup and sandwiches took up a good deal of Lydia's time. Luke seemed to have one or two missions of his own as there were guests staying in the cottage, and so they didn't see much of one another.

Ginny came over on the second

264

afternoon and they chatted over tea and cakes and caught up with all the gossip.

Lydia was just waving goodbye to her when Luke appeared.

'Can we talk?'

She looked at him curiously. 'This sounds serious — what's happened?'

They went into Aunt Mattie's sitting-room.

'I feel it's best that you hear the truth from me. My family have discovered that I've found out who my mother is and — well, I'm afraid it's caused a bit of an upset, as I knew it would.'

'Well, you're a grown man — and surely it's your right to know who your real mother is?'

'Of course, but maybe I've been a bit thoughtless in the way I've gone about things. Anyway, what's done is done.'

He hesitated, and she waited with bated breath as she wondered what he was about to tell her.

'Uncle Joel told me that, while he and Mattie were in Yorkshire, they would be visiting her sister . . . '

'Aunt Janet — well, yes. She's Aunt Mattie's only remaining living relative . . . '

She trailed off as she saw the expression on his face and said incredulously, 'You surely don't mean to tell me that Janet . . . '

'Yes, your Aunt Janet is my mother!'

She stared at him open-mouthed, unable to get her head round what he was telling her.

'How did you? I mean . . . '

He came and sat beside her.

'Uncle Joel and I had a heart-to-heart recently. After all, once I'd discovered my mother's identity, there was no point in trying to pull the wool over my eyes any more, was there?

'He told me that my father and your aunt had been childhood sweethearts and were secretly engaged — and that, at the time my father died, Janet was pregnant but didn't know it.

'She suffered terribly from depression after the accident and was five months' pregnant by the time either she or her parents realised there was a baby on the way.

'Her parents were horrified, and paid for her to go away to a home in the country until after I was born, to avoid any scandal. Attitudes were different then from nowadays.

'Apparently, Janet was incredibly ill when I was born. Her parents wanted me adopted and she really wasn't in any fit state to make any decisions, but she agreed to let my paternal grandmother look after me for a while. By the time she'd recovered, it seems she'd been persuaded to let my Aunt Mary and Uncle Tom bring me up, but the arrangement was that she wasn't to be allowed any contact. And that's why any contact between Robert's brother and Janet's sister was taboo as far as both families were concerned.'

'That seems rather harsh,' Lydia put in.

'As I've said, times were different then. Uncle Joel tells me my mother is a bright lady and was going to university.

As it transpires, she got behind with her studies because of what happened, and ended up training as a teacher a year or so later.'

'Have you — been in touch?' she asked softly.

He shook his head. 'Not as yet, no. I'm not sure what to do. Uncle Joel and Mattie are going to speak to her. You can probably tell me more about her. What's she like? Is she anything like me?'

Lydia thought for a moment. Her Aunt Janet was a taller, slimmer version of Aunt Mattie, and she had taught in the same village school in Yorkshire ever since Lydia could remember.

'She's lovely — rather serious, but she's caring and good-natured and good with children. There's a sadness in her eyes which are brown — like yours. Oh, what a lot of unnecessary suffering there's been all these years! Fancy being persuaded to give her baby away!'

'But I had a truly happy childhood. And I suppose Janet's parents thought what they were doing was right for both of us, at the time.'

'But she didn't attempt to find you?'

'It would have been difficult because both sets of grandparents kept any knowledge of my whereabouts to themselves.'

It was such a sad story. Lydia thought of Aunt Janet who had never married — a spinster lady and highly respected in the community — harbouring such a secret.

'Now I've come to terms with what happened, at long last, and I'm prepared to accept that if it isn't possible to change things, then you just have to move on,' he said quietly. He looked at her and gave her one of his special smiles. 'So, now that you know my questions about your Aunt Mattie and your family weren't for any sinister purpose, can we please begin again?'

Before she realised it, she was in his arms and he was kissing her, stroking her hair and murmuring endearments.

For a few moments, happiness

flooded through her and she responded in a way that left him in no doubt as to her feelings for him, but then his mobile phone rang, disturbing their special moment and, with a muttered exclamation, he pulled away to answer it.

She sat there in a little world of her own for a few moments, until she realised he was talking to Simone!

By the time he'd finished his call, she already had her hand on the doorknob on her way out of the room.

'I think if we're ever going to get any peace and quiet, we'll have to get away from this place,' he told her. 'There are just too many interruptions.'

'Don't bother!' she snapped and stormed off.

* ★ *

For the next couple of days, although it was very difficult, Lydia kept out of Luke's way as much as possible until eventually he cornered her as she was coming from the kitchen and, catching hold of her arm, marched her back inside, closing the door firmly behind them.

'Right, so now you can tell me what I'm supposed to have done? I thought we were getting on just fine but obviously I'm mistaken. If it was the kiss, then I apologise. I must have misread the signals which were coming across loud and clear, so far as I could tell.'

She coloured furiously and shook off his arm.

'You just don't get it, do you? I don't want to take second place in your affections — to be here for you when you're away from her.'

Luke looked completely mystified for a few moments, his brow furrowed in a frown.

'Who exactly are you talking about, Lydia?'

'Surely you don't want me to spell it out for you?' she demanded. 'S-I-M . . .'

'Simone! You can't mean Simone!'

271

He bellowed with laughter which only served to make her angrier still.

'Well, you can't deny she's always ringing you up and Nell told me you were involved with her.'

'That young lady's got a lot to answer for! I told Nell that while I was happy to take her out for an occasional meal, there could never be anything else between us because, apart from being too old for her, quite frankly she just isn't my type, and I already had feelings for someone else. She obviously jumped to the wrong conclusion and concocted this story. You see, Simone is my assistant manager. She's been keeping an eye on things while I've been up here and likes to run things by me before making any major decisions. And now, if that really is all that is worrying your pretty head . . . '

Lydia's eyes were troubled but she had to know the truth, however painful it might be.

'But if it isn't Simone — then there's obviously someone else that you care about.'

'And I'm looking right at her, my darling!'

He caught her in his arms and, this time, she knew that there really was no-one else. He held her close as if he would never let her go.

When the phone rang neither of them stirred but it was very persistent.

Once more the call was for Luke. It wasn't a long call and, when he came off the line, there was a curious mixture of expressions on his face. He sank down on to the sofa.

'That was Janet,' he said, almost in a whisper. 'That was my mother — she wants to see me. It seems that there is another woman in my life after all, Lydia!'

She sat down beside him and put her arms around him. His eyes were moist with emotion and she held him close and stroked his hair and then they kissed again.

273

Later, they went for a walk, hand in hand. 'Any minute now someone will come charging after us to ask for some more teabags or if we can let them have a little butter,' Lydia said.

'That's what running a guesthouse is all about,' he teased. 'I'm beginning to realise it's much more personal than managing a hotel.'

Presently, they sat overlooking a small tarn, catching their breath at the spectacular scenery.

'There are still a couple of things puzzling me even now, Luke,' Lydia told him.

'Then I'll do my best to explain them away, sweetheart.'

She rested in the shelter of his arms. 'Uncle Ted was a comedian and Joel was too. Was that just a coincidence, and did they ever meet up again after Uncle Ted was married to Mattie?'

'Oh, yes. And it wasn't a coincidence that they both went into show business. Ted did a stint once in a London theatre. Joel saw his name and went to

274

see him in his dressing-room afterwards. They went for a drink, chatted over old times and — due to Ted's influence — Joel managed to get to see the producer for an audition. That was the start of his career as a comedian.'

'Did he really never meet up with Mattie again — before now, I mean?'

'I don't think so, but he made a promise to Ted that he would look after her if anything happened to him — and that's exactly what he's done.'

'There were some missing photographs in one of the albums,' she said tentatively.

He reached for his pocket and took out his wallet. 'These you mean? Your aunt gave them to me.'

They were photographs of his parents — Joel's younger brother Robert and Aunt Janet, in happier times.

As they began to walk back towards Hill House, Luke said, 'I asked you the other day if you believed in love at first sight?'

She nodded, her heart thumping

wildly at his closeness.

'You see, Lydia, I fell in love with you from the moment you walked into the dining-room at Hill House on that first morning in May.'

His brown eyes locked with her blue-grey ones.

'So, dare I ask you how you feel about me?'

Lydia reached up and touched his dear face, tracing its outline, and then their lips met and he got his answer.

'So what about you?' he asked, as they walked hand in hand by the tarn. 'My life seems to be sorting itself out but you've still got your problem with Trent leaving the studio.'

She shrugged her shoulders. 'I could always rent out the studio and come up here to work for a while. Anthea's asked me to join her in Keswick, but then I'd be farther away from you in London than ever . . . '

'Sweetheart, if it means finding work in a hotel up here, then that's what I'll do. But perhaps you want some space

276

— some time to yourself to think about things.'

She smiled up at him. 'Do you?'

He shook his head. 'I'm thirty-six — rather older than you and I've waited until now for the girl of my dreams to come along. I don't need to wait any longer because I'm absolutely certain that she's you.'

Her heart was singing as he took her in his arms. 'I love you, Luke.'

'Enough to marry me?'

Her heartbeat quickened. 'Oh, yes, Luke, quite enough. You see, I'm absolutely certain too!'

Her eyes danced with merriment.

'And if we could arrange the wedding for the very near future, then we could go to Rome for our honeymoon!'

'We'll discuss that later! But first things first!'

This time there were no interruptions, and when he caught her in his arms, their kiss was long and lingering and extremely satisfying.

We do hope that you have enjoyed reading this large print book.

Did you know that all of our titles are available for purchase?

We publish a wide range of high quality large print books including:
Romances, Mysteries, Classics
General Fiction
Non Fiction and Westerns

Special interest titles available in large print are:
The Little Oxford Dictionary
Music Book, Song Book
Hymn Book, Service Book

Also available from us courtesy of Oxford University Press:
Young Readers' Dictionary
(large print edition)
Young Readers' Thesaurus
(large print edition)

For further information or a free brochure, please contact us at:
Ulverscroft Large Print Books Ltd.,
The Green, Bradgate Road, Anstey,
Leicester, LE7 7FU, England.
Tel: (00 44) **0116 236 4325**
Fax: (00 44) **0116 234 0205**

Other titles in the
Linford Romance Library:

DUET IN LOW KEY

Doris Rae

In their quiet Highland village, the minister, David Sinclair, and his wife Morag, await the return of their daughter Bridget from convalescence. But a newcomer to the village causes Morag some consternation. Ledoux, big and flamboyant, is a Canadian forester, and has caused a stir locally. Morag fears that Ledoux, at a loose end in the quiet community, might make a play for their gentle and innocent daughter — and the potential for scandal would never do . . .

ONLY A DAY AWAY

Chrissie Loveday

When Sally is offered a position in New Zealand, she sees it as the opportunity of a lifetime. Unfortunately, her mother doesn't share her view — and neither does her fiancé. Sadly, she hands back his ring and looks to an uncertain future. When Adam arrives in her life though, along with a gorgeous little boy, everything becomes even more complicated. But New Zealand works its own brand of magic, and for Sally an unexpected, whole new life is beginning . . .

WHENEVER YOU ARE NEAR

Jeanrose Buczynski

After her break up from a disastrous engagement, Sienna Churchill is ready to make the most of life again and flies to Spain to work as a travel rep with a friend. However, six months later she returns home to her father's farm — and makes a shocking discovery when a ghost from the past reappears . . .

YESTERDAY'S SECRETS

Janet Thomas

Recently divorced archaeologist Jo Kingston comes home to Cornwall with her daughter Sophie to live with her father. When her old 'flame', Nick Angove, is injured on a dig Jo takes over, but faces fierce resentment from him. Then, intriguingly, human bones are found and the police become involved. Nick is injured, apparently when disobeying orders, but actually in saving Sophie's life. And as the truth emerges, they begin to acknowledge that their former love has never really died.